Faith wondered how long she'd be able to stay.

Then a horrible thought hit her. When Luke left, she and his mother would be vulnerable and unprotected. She couldn't do that to his mother. She'd have to leave when Luke did. Her shoulders slumped as exhaustion settled. She didn't want to think about moving on just yet.

The creaking sound of a door next to hers opening heralded Luke's arrival.

She didn't want to be attracted to Luke, and she didn't need another man in her life. She had more problems than she could handle. Like keeping herself from becoming too attached to Luke's family, like protecting these good people and like planning her next move.

With a groan, she turned off the light. As tired as she was, she knew it would be a long time before her mind could banish the images of the cowboy next door.

Books by Terri Reed

Love Inspired Suspense

Strictly Confidential
*Double Deception
Beloved Enemy
Her Christmas Protector
*Double Jeopardy
*Double Cross
*Double Threat Christmas
Her Last Chance
Chasing Shadows
Covert Pursuit
Holiday Havoc
"Yuletide Sanctuary"
Daughter of Texas
†*The Innocent Witness*
†*The Secret Heiress*
The Deputy's Duty
†*The Doctor's Defender*

Love Inspired

Love Comes Home
A Sheltering Love
A Sheltering Heart
A Time of Hope
Giving Thanks for Baby
Treasure Creek Dad

*The McClains
†Protection Specialists

TERRI REED

At an early age Terri Reed discovered the wonderful world of fiction and declared she would one day write a book. Now she is fulfilling that dream and enjoys writing for Love Inspired Books. Her second book, *A Sheltering Love,* was a 2006 RITA® Award finalist and a 2005 National Readers' Choice Award finalist. Her book *Strictly Confidential,* book five in the Faith at the Crossroads continuity series, took third place in the 2007 American Christian Fiction Writers Book of the Year Award, and *Her Christmas Protector* took third place in 2008. She is an active member of both Romance Writers of America and American Christian Fiction Writers. She resides in the Pacific Northwest with her college-sweetheart husband, two wonderful children and an array of critters. When not writing, she enjoys spending time with her family and friends, gardening and playing with her dogs.

You can write to Terri at P.O. Box 19555 Portland, OR 97280. Visit her on the web at www.loveinspiredauthors.com, leave comments on her blog, www.ladiesofsuspense.blogspot.com, or email her at terrireed@sterling.net.

Her
Christmas
Protector

Terri Reed

Love Inspired

Recycling programs
for this product may
not exist in your area.

™ LOVE INSPIRED BOOKS

ISBN-13: 978-0-373-78743-2

HER CHRISTMAS PROTECTOR

www.LoveInspiredBooks.com

Printed in U.S.A.

The fear of man brings a snare, but whoever trusts in the Lord shall be safe.
—*Proverbs* 29:25

To my mother, Dorothy. I love you.

ONE

The scent of pine evoked memories of better times, times before…

The doors of the bus swooshed closed. The hulking vehicle rambled away, leaving Faith Delange in a wake of acrid exhaust.

Stifling a cough, she set her bags on the ground and tugged her wool coat tighter against the December chill. Though nothing could ever guard her against the isolation and fear of being found.

A "Help Wanted" sign hanging in the window of a little diner caught her attention and her stomach growled, spurring her onward. Her leather-soled shoes slipped slightly on patches of ice and sloshed in the dirty snow.

A clear, blue sky made a perfect backdrop for tall evergreens and the rustic little town nestled amid the snow-dusted greenery. In the distance, majestic mountains rose above the trees as if stretching toward heaven. Her gaze took in the town, which looked to be a refurbished antique of the old west decorated with holiday cheer. A sense of well-being swirled around her. A spark of hope leaped to life deep within her soul.

Faith liked what she saw. Here, she could be anybody. Here, she could be safe, if only long enough to rest and eat.

Maybe here, God might answer her prayers. The beginnings of a smile tugged at the corners of her mouth.

With the side of her hip, she pushed open the door of the restaurant and walked into a replica of an old dining car. Over the striped wallpaper hung festive cutouts. A small Christmas tree sat on the counter near the cash register. A bright yellow box with the word "toys" blazoned across the front sat overflowing with wrapped presents to the right of the door. Booths upholstered in red vinyl lined the walls. In the corner, a jukebox played a slow country melody, the words of love and loss bringing a pang to Faith's heart.

A frazzled, gray-haired waitress smiled from across the room. "Come on in, honey." The waitress wiped a hand across the skirt of her apron, adding another greasy stain to the front. "Sit where you'd like."

Every head in the diner swiveled in Faith's direction. She dropped her gaze to the floor and wished people would go back to what they were doing. She just wanted to blend in, be another faceless body.

Who was she kidding? Not only was she a stranger in this small community, but she looked awful, having worn the same clothes for the last three days.

The smell of bacon drifted past her nose, reminding her of her goal. Food and a job. But the last open booth seemed a mile away from where she stood.

She tightened her grip on her tattered suitcases and started forward just as an older, grizzled man in a plaid shirt vacated a spot at the counter. Moving quickly, Faith claimed the stool and set her suitcases on the floor at her feet.

In her peripheral vision she noticed the man to her right and his openly curious stare. She tilted her head away and picked up the menu.

The waitress wiped down the counter. "What can I get for you, dear?"

Her mouth watering and her stomach cramping with hunger, Faith succumbed to the temptation to order a full meal. "I'll have the eggs Benedict, please." She set down the menu. "And coffee."

"Ethel, here, brews the best coffee in the whole state," the man stated.

Faith nodded her acknowledgement but kept her gaze forward. She didn't talk to strangers. Especially men.

Ethel beamed. "You're a charmer, L.C. Your order will be right up, dear." The waitress moved away with a spring in her step.

The warmth of the diner seeped into Faith's skin and her coat became too much. She shrugged it down her shoulders and released her left arm from the sleeve. Gingerly, she tried to push the right sleeve down without having to raise her arm.

"Here, let me," the man, L.C., offered as he reached for her coat.

Faith jerked back at the unexpected move. She

stared at him. He had close-cropped dark hair and a ruggedly handsome face with a strong jawline. The slight bump along the ridge of his nose gave his face character, and she wondered how he'd acquired the break. His clean-shaven cheeks barely hinted at the dark shadow she guessed would appear by the end of the day. Dark eyebrows slashed over the bluest eyes she'd ever seen.

Just because he was handsome didn't mean she could trust him. She knew better than most what evil could lurk behind a beautiful facade.

"I'm sorry. I didn't mean to startle you," he said, holding up calloused hands.

"Th…that's okay."

"May I?" he asked and nodded his head toward her arm.

Not wanting to draw more attention, she slowly nodded. One of his big hands caught the end of her sleeve, his fingers lightly brushing against the back of her hand, setting off a maelstrom of tingles up her arm. His other hand grasped the collar of her coat. In a smooth motion he slipped the coat down her arm. Faith winced slightly as her shoulder moved.

"Did I hurt you?" L.C.'s rich, mellow voice held a note of concern.

She swallowed and tried to find her voice. "Old injury."

"Would you like to hang your jacket up?" He motioned toward a row of hooks on the wall near the entryway.

"No, thanks." She took the coat and laid it across one of her bags.

He turned his attention back to his breakfast. Faith studied him from the corner of her eye. He wore dusty cowboy boots, faded jeans and a blue denim shirt. A cowboy? In Oregon? She'd pictured the mountains of the northwest full of lumberjacks, not cowboys.

Ethel placed a large plateful of steaming hot food in front of Faith. Faith's stomach reacted to the aroma with a loud rumble.

At the man's deep chuckle, a sheepish smile touched her lips. "I'm hungry."

"So I heard." He flashed a grin.

Heat crept up her neck.

Ethel leaned her hip against the counter in front of the man, drawing his attention. "How's your mother coming along?"

He sighed. "Better. Reva's been tending to her, but Mom isn't happy about it. She wants me to find someone else to come in and stay with her."

Ethel snorted. "I don't blame her. Reva would be the last person I'd want hovering over me. She'd be enough to bring on another heart attack."

Faith glanced at L.C. to see how he'd take Ethel's disparaging remarks about this Reva person. His expression remained calm and composed. So not like other men she'd known in her life.

Luke shrugged. "Reva means well. Though, I came into town to put an ad in the paper for someone else to help out."

Faith almost choked on her food. He needed someone to help with his mother. For one insane moment, she almost said she'd take the job. But she needed a way to get cash fast. Just what the job in the diner would offer.

"Now, you tell her hello for me. Tell her we miss her at choir practice and I'll try to get out to the ranch this week for a visit."

"I will, Ethel, thanks."

Ethel turned to Faith. "How's your breakfast, dear?"

Faith swallowed before answering. "Wonderful." And to the man beside her she added, "And the coffee is great."

"Told you so." He gave her a crooked grin, knocking the breath from her lungs. As a teenager, she'd dreamed of smiles like his.

She'd also dreamed of a happy, normal marriage. Now all she had were nightmares.

"L.C.?"

He extended his hand. "Luke Campbell, at your service, Miss…"

Tentatively, she took his hand. The kiss of the sun had tanned his calloused fingers, a stark contrast to the paleness of her own hand. "Faith Delange."

She bit back a gasp of anxiety at giving out her real name. Having used so many aliases over the last three months she sometimes forgot who she was supposed to be.

But he'd distracted her.

A big no-no.

She couldn't let her guard down. Not for a second. She could never be sure who would be the one to give her away.

"Well, Faith, what brings you to Sisters?"

He leaned back and eyed her with an intensity that brought a heated flush to her cheeks. Her heart beat erratically at the probing question. "I'm just passing through."

"That's too bad." He cocked his head to one side and studied her. "Where are you headed?"

Good question. She didn't want to say, where I can't be found, so she shrugged. "I'm just traveling around, seeing America." That sounded innocuous enough.

"Really?" His gaze shifted to her suitcases on the floor.

She asked quickly, "What do you do, Mr. Campbell?"

"Please, call me Luke."

Her gaze dropped to her plate. "Luke."

"I…well, for the moment, I'm a rancher."

"Why just for the moment?"

"I'm a captain in the army. My father recently passed away and my mother suffered a heart attack not long after. Thankfully, I had enough unused leave to come home and help."

Her hand went to her heart. "I'm so sorry."

"It's been hard." Luke noticed the delicate shape of her fingers, fine-boned and petite. The kind of fingers meant for diamonds. Hers were bare.

He could tell she'd been traveling hard. Her wrinkled clothes looked well-worn, and the dark circles beneath her eyes told him she needed rest. He studied her face, liking the high cheekbones, wide, generous mouth and catlike eyes. Those eyes shifted ever-so-slightly toward the door. Luke twisted around to see what she found so fascinating, but there was nothing there. "Are you waiting for someone?"

"No."

"Are you alone, then?"

She stared hard at him for a moment before slowly answering, "Yes."

"Where are you staying?"

"Oh, I'm not." She spoke quickly, "I'll be catching the next bus out." She pushed a strand of blond hair behind her ear.

He shouldn't care. He wasn't staying much longer himself. But there was something vulnerable about her that didn't sit well. "Wouldn't it be a good idea to stop and stay in one place for a while? Sisters has a lot to offer."

She glanced at him sharply and wiped daintily at her mouth with a napkin. "I can see a lot from a bus window."

"Must get terribly uncomfortable."

She shrugged.

"How long do you plan to keep traveling?"

"As long as it takes."

"Where to next?"

She thought for a moment. "Alaska."

"As in tundra?"

She gave him a pointed look. "You ask a lot of questions."

He grinned. "Guilty as charged." People tended to open up if the right question was asked. Sometimes it took a lot of questions. "I'm a curious man."

She leaned in close. "Haven't you heard the one about curiosity killing the cat?"

Following her movement, he leaned closer. "Will my curiosity kill me?"

Abruptly, she sat back. Her expression took on a pained, faraway look. "It could, I suppose. I really don't know."

"Want to tell me about it?"

Her expression became guarded. "About what?"

Every nerve ending went on alert. She was hiding something. Luke stifled the urge to press and ran a hand through his hair. He didn't need this. Her. He had enough guilt for not being there for his father to take on another person's problems.

Ethel stopped before them. "Would either of you like anything else?"

Faith's expression changed and became hopeful. "Do you have pie?"

At least she had good taste and a healthy appetite. "Good choice."

Faith liked the way Luke's eyes crinkled at the corners. But his questions still made her uncomfortable and she was thankful he let the subject drop. The last thing she needed was to have someone probing into her life. Making judgments or, worse yet, pitying her.

He pulled out his billfold from his back pocket and laid cash down on the counter.

"Here's our homemade apple pie," Ethel announced, setting the pie on the counter before moving away.

Luke rose and took a thick brown, shearling-lined leather coat from the hook and placed a traditional cowboy hat on his head. With an engaging grin he tipped the brim. "Faith, nice meeting you. Have a safe trip to Alaska."

Safety. If only she had a guarantee she'd find it in the tundra, she'd actually head that way. "Thanks."

As she watched him walk out, a familiar sense of loneliness assailed her. Only now it was more pronounced. For a moment, talking to the man, she'd felt normal. Mr. Campbell had been kind and thoughtful. Something she'd found too little of lately. Would she ever get used to the isolation?

"How's that pie?" Ethel asked, as she refilled Faith's coffee mug.

"Delicious," she replied. "I…I wanted to…inquire about the job?"

Ethel's expression went blank.

"The 'Help Wanted' sign in the window," Faith prompted.

"Oh, lands sakes." Ethel shook her head. "I'm sorry, dear. That should have been taken down two days ago."

Disappointment rolled through Faith with the force of a thunderstorm. "Oh, I see."

"I'll go take care of that sign right now." Ethel hurried away.

Setting down her fork, Faith pulled open her handbag and brought out a small leather pouch. She tugged out the bills and let the change fall to the table. She didn't think she'd have enough left after she paid her bill to buy another bus ticket.

Okay, time to regroup. The waitressing job wouldn't have been an ideal choice anyway. She'd be too visible here, too easy to find. The town was too small.

She scoffed at the irony her life had become. Instead of tipping the server, she was the one in need of the tip. Her grandfather would be so disgusted. And he'd left her all that money. But she couldn't dip into her inheritance without throwing up a big red flag.

Pushing away the pie plate, she dropped her head into her hands. *Oh, God, please help me.*

What was the point? God had abandoned her long ago. She supposed her grandfather's steadfast belief kept her wanting to believe. But so far God hadn't heard her prayers.

Lifting her head, she stared through blurry eyes at the money lying on the table. What was she to do?

An image of Luke drifted across her consciousness and she recalled his conversation with Ethel. He needed someone to care for his mother. An idea blossomed in the back of her mind.

He didn't exactly say he was looking for a nurse, just someone to help his mother recover.

She could do that.

After all, she'd been the one to care for her grandfather after he suffered his heart attack. She'd watched the team of nurses come and go, seen the services they'd provided. She'd jumped right in when the nurses had refused to stay.

She had owed her grandfather that for having taken her in after her parents died. Gerald Emerson Delange had been a Bible-thumping, judgmental and unyielding man. But she'd loved him and no one could be as difficult to care for as he'd been.

Oh, yes, she could care for Luke's mother.

But would it be a wise choice?

She wouldn't be visible, she'd have a place to stay and the job would probably pay decently. If no one knew she was there, maybe she'd even be safe for a while.

She stretched the aching muscles in her back. She couldn't go on like this. Fatigue was making her mind fuzzy, not to mention her dwindling funds. And the longer she stayed in the open, the more chance she'd be found.

What choice did she have?

Faith paid her bill, gathered her belongings, and hurried from the diner to find Luke.

She caught a glimpse of him as he turned the corner, disappearing behind a building a block down the street. Even from a distance he made a striking picture. Instead of the expected easy-rolling gait of a cowboy, he walked with a purposeful stride. Head up and shoulders back. Very controlled. In fact, everything about Luke spoke of a forthright and self-controlled man.

I'm a captain in the army.

She had the feeling that with Luke you got what you saw. Faith liked that. It was so opposite of what she'd lived with for so long.

Desperate to catch him before he disappeared altogether, she jogged down the sidewalk, her bags jostling at her sides.

She turned the corner as Luke climbed into a dark green Bronco. An instant later, the engine roared to life. He backed his vehicle out of the parking place, the tires crunching on the snow-covered gravel. Faith dropped her bags and ran toward him.

"Luke! Luke, wait!"

The Bronco screeched to a stop. Luke rolled down his window. "Faith, are you okay?"

His deep voice washed over her, smoothing the rough edges of her nerves.

Nodding, she blinked up at him. "I…I wanted to ask you something."

He gave her a curious stare. "Ask away."

Anxiety threatened to wrap itself around her throat, but she bolstered her courage and plunged ahead. "I'd like to apply for that job you mentioned earlier."

A confused frown marred his brow. "Job?"

Faith took a deep breath. "For your mother. The helper you needed."

"I thought you were just passing through?"

"I changed my mind. The country air agrees with me." She breathed in deep, the cold air filling her lungs and making her cough. It was either the air or she was losing her mind.

She probably was nuts to be doing this, but would she be found in this out-of-the-way town in the middle of the Oregon Mountains? And on a ranch?

No, she didn't think so. She was ninety-nine percent sure she'd be safe.

She'd worry about the other one percent later.

TWO

Hire her, Luke thought to himself immediately, and then heard himself say, "You're hired."

Her eyes rounded in surprise. "Just like that?"

Luke hesitated. He knew next to nothing about this woman and yet, when he looked into her eyes, the haunted expression that had bothered him earlier seemed to recede. "Just like that."

"I'll…get my bags."

"Here, let me," Luke offered as he opened the door. But she was already hurrying away.

Luke drummed his fingers on the door. *Okay, Lord. I trust You know what You're doing. Whatever You have planned, I'm with You.*

Still, he couldn't shake the unsettled knot in the pit of his stomach.

As Faith approached, Luke climbed out from behind the wheel and took her bags. He put them in the back and then helped her into the rig. "You travel light for someone who's been out touring the country."

"Easier to pack up and go."

Luke climbed back behind the wheel and wondered what made her need to "pack up and go."

He clamped his jaw tight. Why couldn't God have provided some nice grandmotherly type, someone he could easily dismiss from his mind?

Luke slanted Faith a glance as he pulled out onto the street. Something about the way she held herself spoke of a quiet strength he found appealing. He wasn't immune to her physical charms, either.

He liked the straight line of her nose and the stubbornness of her jaw. Her blond hair swung about her shoulders and he could almost imagine the feel of the silken strands gliding across his palm.

Resolutely, he shook the sensation away. He really didn't need this.

Suddenly, Faith moved, throwing herself on the floor and he nearly careened into a building. He eased up on the gas pedal. "What are you doing?"

Her hunted expression reappeared, making her look wide-eyed and scared. "I…think my…ear…earring fell out," she stammered and patted the floorboards.

For several seconds she continued to search the floor.

There'd been no jewelry adorning her ears. Interesting. "Find it?"

"Yes." She attempted to sit up but her purse went flying to the floor, scattering paraphernalia at their feet. Diving down, she retrieved her goods.

Luke could have sworn she'd nudged her purse off the seat on purpose. Curiosity burned in his gut. "Room and board."

He glanced down at her bent head. He noticed one hand held her purse while the other put air into the purse's opening. His curiosity cranked up a notch and his brows drew together.

She peeked at him through a veil of blond hair. "Excuse me?"

She was acting so…odd. Luke forced his attention on the road ahead of them. "I said, room and board. Plus two-hundred dollars a week."

"That sounds perfect." Her muffled voice held relief.

They passed through town and he waved at several people. Then the realization hit him. She didn't want anyone to see her leaving with him.

Why?

Luke turned the truck onto the road leading to his parents' ranch. "We're out of town. You're safe now."

Faith started and sat up. Her face flushed a deep crimson. "What do you mean?"

He nodded toward the floor. "You find everything?"

"Huh? Oh, yes. Thanks." She turned away from him, her hands clasped into a tight knot.

Seeing her knuckles turn white, he felt the need to assure her and calm her fears. "Relax, Faith. It's going to be okay."

The fearful expression in her eyes told him she wasn't convinced.

A little small talk might ease the situation. "Where are you from?"

"Back east."

"Back east is a big place," he stated with wry amusement.

One corner of her mouth lifted. "New York."

He arched an eyebrow. "It's a big state."

She slanted a glance his way. "Yes. It is."

He'd bet she came from money. The graceful table manners she'd displayed and her cultured speech oozed private school, which only left him more intrigued.

"The countryside is so beautiful and peaceful," she commented, then asked, "Have you lived here your whole life?"

"Born and raised." He didn't mention he'd left at eighteen and only recently returned.

"How long ago did your mother have her heart attack?"

"Two weeks." He'd wanted a nurse to care for his mother just in case she suffered another attack, but the doctor had assured him she would be back to normal soon. All she needed was rest and a little exercise. And someone constantly making sure she was doing just that. Someone besides Reva May Scott.

"What does your family think of your see-America jaunt?" he asked.

She pressed her lips together and shrugged. "Who's Reva?"

She was good at changing the subject. "That's a complicated question."

He thought for a moment how best to answer. "Her father and my dad were good friends. When her mother took off after she was born, her dad started drinking. My dad tried to step in as much as possible for them."

"That was generous. So you two are like siblings then?"

He let out a short laugh. Reva would disagree. "Yeah, something like that."

"I take it from what you told Ethel, Reva and your mother don't get along."

"No, they don't. Mom tried real hard with her when Reva was a little girl, but..." He shrugged. "Reva would never accept my mom."

"That's too bad," Faith commented, her expression thoughtful. "I hope your mom will be okay with me coming home with you."

Letting up on the gas, the Bronco slowed as he turned onto the gravel drive. "I wouldn't be bringing you home if I didn't think I was making the right decision."

She turned away to stare out the window. Stretching before them in wild splendor was his family's five-hundred acres. At the end of the drive sat a two-story farmhouse, flanked on either side by a pair of large, red barns, one of which had four apartments on the second floor. A paddock and corral sat off to the right side of the barn while the other side was open grazing land with sage brush and bare trees sticking up through the layer of snow.

"Oh my, is this your ranch?" Her voice filled with awe.

"Welcome to the Circle C," Luke said with pride.

Faith twisted to look back the way they'd come.

"The road is very visible. I suppose you can see cars coming long before they arrive?"

"Yes."

"Good." She sat forward. "That's good. You're pretty safe out here."

He arched a brow. "What are you afraid of?"

A huge caramel-colored animal ran along the fence.

"You raise llamas?" She turned her curious gaze on him and left his question unanswered. Again.

The depths of her hazel eyes pulled at him. He debated pressing for an answer, but there would be time enough later. "Llamas, cattle and horses."

"I've never seen a llama up close."

"They make great pets. We raise them for their coats. Raising llamas is a hobby for my mother. She used to show them, but then people started wanting to buy them so we expanded the operation.

"Our stable is small compared to others who solely raise llamas. Few people realize that Sisters is the llama capital of the United States."

"Why here?"

"Central Oregon's climate is similar to that of Peru, where llamas originate. Sisters is ideal, open and temperate."

"I agree. This place is perfect."

Luke had a feeling she meant more than just the climate. He stopped in front of the house and his golden retriever bounded up to the Bronco. Opening the door, he received a series of wet dog kisses. "Whoa, girl. It's good to see you, too."

Suddenly, the dog's ears perked up and her head

lifted. She dashed out of view before Luke could react, and Faith became the recipient of the retriever's sloppy love.

Luke rounded the corner of the Bronco and stopped. Faith kneeled with her arms around his dog. The sight made him smile.

"She's beautiful. What's her name?"

"Brandy."

"Luke, what's going on?" A female voice brought all three heads around to face the house. Reva stood on the porch, her hands on her hips and her red lips pressed into a stiff line.

Irritation pulsed through Luke, but he shook off the feeling. It was only natural Reva would be curious, but her question seemed more accusatory than not. He glanced at Faith, who now stood with her hands clasped together and a polite smile plastered on her face.

He silently retrieved Faith's bags and guided Faith toward the house. Brandy, he noted, stayed close to Faith.

"Who is this?" Reva asked, her eyes wide, as she looked Faith up and down.

"A guest," he answered, wishing Reva wouldn't act so territorially.

Brandy growled then let out a loud bark. Luke understood the dog's urge to protect Faith. He felt the same protective instincts roaring to life in his veins.

"Tell me what I want to hear," Vince Palmero demanded of the man on the phone.

Bob Grady cleared his throat. "Sorry, boss. We lost her trail in Portland, Oregon."

Vince clenched his fist. "How incompetent can you be?"

"We'll get her. I've got men combing the city and checking the trains, buses and airport."

"Time is running out. Find her!"

Vince slammed down the receiver and pushed back his leather chair from the expansive mahogany desk. He tugged on the collar of his Italian handmade dress shirt feeling as choked with rage as if the Armani striped tie around his neck was being cinched tight. He couldn't believe she'd done this to him. If he didn't find her and bring her back soon, his whole life would go down the tubes.

He stared at the framed photo on his sidebar. A stunning smile and hazel eyes burned into his mind. He'd loved her, offered her everything and she'd betrayed him.

She'd pay. Oh, yes. When he found her, she'd pay.

Faith's sweaty palm stuck to the banister. She wiped her hand on her pant leg as she followed Luke and Reva up the stairs to his mother's room. Although the initial meeting with Reva went well—the woman had been pleasant enough—Faith could tell that Reva didn't like having another woman in what she obviously considered her domain.

As they'd passed through the living room, Faith noted the lack of Christmas decorations. Maybe these people didn't celebrate the birth of Jesus. Whether they did or not wasn't relative to her safety.

Luke knocked on a door at the end of the hallway. Little butterflies fluttered in the pit of Faith's stomach. If Luke's mother didn't like her, then what would she do? The ranch represented a security she'd only hoped of. She wanted to stay. *Please, oh, please, dear Lord, let her like me.*

At his mother's muffled, "Come in," Luke pushed open the door and stepped aside so Reva and Faith could enter. As Faith passed him, he gave her a reassuring smile and some of the butterflies in her stomach danced for an altogether different reason.

A blast of heat hit her in the face as she stepped into the room. The bedroom was at least ten degrees warmer than the rest of the house. Sweat beads broke out and trickled down Faith's neck. The dark-haired woman lying on the canopied oak bed looked wilted and weak beneath the heavy covers pulled up to her chin.

"Ugh, Reva, it's hot in here," Luke exclaimed. "I've told you a hundred times not to touch the thermostat."

"But, Luke, honey, the doctor said she wasn't to get a chill."

In long strides, Luke moved to one window and yanked it open. Almost immediately a cooling breeze entered the room.

"Oh, that feels wonderful." Mrs. Campbell sighed. "I kept asking her to turn down the heat, but she wouldn't listen to me."

Luke paused in the act of pulling the quilt off his mother and looked at Reva. The color of his eyes had darkened to a steely blue and his jaw tightened in anger. Faith stepped back.

"I was only doing what I thought best. She's still recovering from her ordeal," Reva said defensively.

"The way she makes it sound, I'm still knocking on death's door," Luke's mother muttered.

"It's only been two weeks. You know—"

"Enough, Reva."

Luke's command abruptly stopped Reva midwhine. She made a face and sat on the edge of a small desk by the window.

Faith marveled that at least one grown man was mature enough to contain his anger.

"Mom, I have someone here I'd like you to meet." Luke's voice softened.

The eager-to-please tone and the way his voice dropped a notch brought a pang to Faith's heart. This big man loved his mother and it showed. She'd loved her parents like that. If only they were still alive.

He motioned for Faith to step closer.

"This is Faith. I've hired her to help care for you."

Faith approached the bed. The gentle eyes regarding her made her think of her own mother. It had been years since anyone had looked at her with such kindness. She knew instantly she'd like the older woman.

Taking the offered hand, she noticed Mrs. Campbell's skin felt hot and clammy against her palm. "Mrs. Campbell, Luke tells me you're recovering from a heart attack. My grandfather suffered an attack and I cared for him. I—I hope you'll allow me to care for you."

"Please, call me Dottie. I'm sure we'll get along just fine."

From behind her, Faith heard Reva snort in disbelief. She turned to stare at Reva. Such disrespect was reprehensible.

"Reva, please," Luke warned.

Studying her nails, Reva said, "Luke, dear, the housekeeping still needs to be done. Or are you expecting her to do that, too?"

"No, I'm not expecting Faith to do the housekeeping."

"Good." Reva hopped off the edge of the desk and stood. "I'm sure Blake would be happy to know I'm helping out. I'll just stay on and do the housekeeping."

Faith glanced at Luke. His annoyance was evident in the creases along his brow. Turning his gaze to his mother, he raised a brow as if to ask what she thought. Dottie grimaced with a shrug.

Suddenly, Reva was standing close, pinning Faith against the bed. Trying to gracefully disengage herself from Dottie's hand, Faith shifted to allow Reva more room. Dottie's grip tightened and for a second Faith thought she saw a trace of apprehension in the older woman's blue eyes. She guessed there was more going on between the two women than met the eye.

Though the danger was minimal, the familiar need to protect rose sharply. Patting Dottie's hand reassuringly, Faith stood her ground, becoming a physical barrier between Dottie and Reva.

"Your dad promised me I'd have a place here,

Luke. He did consider me a part of the family, especially after you took off."

The muscles in Luke's jaw visibly tightened. "My father and I came to an understanding long ago." Glancing at his mother, he asked, "Mom? This is your house now."

"If she wants to do the housekeeping, I suppose that's fine," Dottie muttered.

Luke gave a curt nod. "Fine. Just stick to the housekeeping, Reva."

"Of course, dear."

Faith noticed the small, triumphant gleam in Reva's gray eyes. She decided she didn't like the woman very much. She would have to be careful and keep her distance. Faith couldn't trust that Reva wouldn't look for an opportunity to get rid of her.

"Do you smell something burning?" Dottie struggled to sit up. Luke immediately reached to help her.

"Oh, my word! My casserole," Reva exclaimed. "There's something wrong with that oven," she muttered as she headed for the door. "It's forever burning things."

"There's nothing wrong with my oven," Dottie groused at Reva's retreating back. "I've never burned anything in it."

"Of course not, mother." Luke's smile reflected in his eyes.

Dottie smiled back, and for a moment, the two silently communicated, their bond evident. Feeling like an intruder, Faith moved to the desk and ran a hand over the polished wood.

Deep inside, she felt a familiar emptiness. She

would give anything to have someone love her the way Luke loved his mother. In her heart she longed for children, a family. But the possibility of having them was out of reach. She could be discovered at any time, and then what? A shudder racked her body.

Picking up the pitcher that sat on the desk, she poured a glass of water and carried it back to the bed. "Would you like some water, Dottie?"

"Thank you, dear." Dottie smiled and took the glass. "Sit and tell me about you."

Faith pulled up a chair. She couldn't very well tell Dottie the truth. So she did what she normally did and changed the subject. "You have a very nice home, Dottie. I noticed several good antique pieces."

Dottie's face lit up. "You know antiques? How wonderful."

A safe subject. Thank goodness. Faith smiled. "Yes, I do. You have good quality pieces."

"Well, if you ladies will excuse me, I'll go get some work done." Luke kissed Dottie's cheek.

"You go on, son. We'll be just fine." Dottie settled back with a grin.

To Faith, Luke said, "If you need anything, I'll be downstairs in the office. First door on your right at the bottom of the stairs."

"Thanks."

"Sure." He ran a hand over his short hair and for a moment just stood there staring at her.

Faith raised a questioning brow.

"See you later." He smiled before sauntering from the room.

"That's the first genuine smile I've seen from Luke since he's come home."

"Come home?" Faith asked, still staring at the spot where he'd disappeared through the door, feeling a little unsettled.

"Luke's a captain in the army," Dottie announced with obvious pride in her son.

"Right." Faith smiled at Dottie.

Dottie continued, "He graduated top of his class at West Point. I'm very proud of my son. He followed his dreams."

West Point. Impressive. "I'm…familiar with the school. My grandfather's house sat on the opposite bank of the Hudson River. From the top-floor window we could see part of the academy. Had I been born a boy, my grandfather would have insisted I attend West Point rather than my mother's alma mater, Cornell."

"I'm sure your grandfather was very proud of you. Blake didn't want Luke to go. It caused a rift in their relationship for years."

"That's too bad." Faith hoped the rift had been mended before Blake's death, but she thought it tactless to ask.

As if reading her unspoken thought, Dottie said, "Luckily they patched things up between them a few years ago. Blake was very proud of Luke, too."

"Was Luke able to see his father before he passed on?" Faith asked gently.

"Yes, thankfully." Her expression became troubled. "He wasn't supposed to stay this long but…I had my attack and…well, Blake's health had deteriorated over the last couple of years, so the ranch had been neglected for the most part."

Dottie paused to take a deep breath. "The hands that stayed on have kept things going, but it was Blake who made sure the upkeep and repairs were taken care of. Dear Blake just couldn't give up control. Not even when it became impossible for him to do more than sit and watch."

Compassion filled Faith. From her own experience with caring for her grandfather she knew how hard it was to watch someone you love die. Especially when that person was as strong-willed as her grandfather had been, and as Blake must have been. Faith held the older woman's hand. "I'm so sorry for your loss."

"Thank you, dear. I take comfort in knowing Blake's with Jesus and someday we will be together again."

Conviction shone bright in Dottie's blue eyes, like beacons of light directing the way.

Faith blinked back sudden tears. She wished desperately that she could be as assured of her own place in heaven and to be reunited with her family. But why would God take her to live with Him when He'd shown no interest in her on earth?

Dottie gave her hand a gentle squeeze. "Are you feeling okay?"

Faith cleared her throat before speaking. "Yes. Fine, thank you."

"You must forgive me if I tend to rattle on."

Thinking it infinitely better for Dottie to talk, she said, "Oh, please. Rattle all you'd like."

And she did. For Faith, the next couple of hours were a breath of fresh air. They discovered many common interests such as antiques, art, theater and cooking. And Faith was more than happy to exhaust all subjects except the topic of her own life. Soon Dottie was yawning and her eyelids drooping.

"Goodness, I don't think I've had this much to talk about in years." Dottie beamed as Faith helped her settle back into a reclined position.

"Nor have I." Faith fluffed the pillows beneath Dottie's head. "You need some rest now. I'll come back later and we can pick up where we left off."

Dottie's eyes were already closed. Unsure what she should do now, Faith wandered over to a window and stood gazing out at the expanse of land that made up the Circle C Ranch. Never in her wildest dreams had she thought she'd find sanctuary in the home of a cowboy.

Could it be possible that God was watching out for her after all?

THREE

"Have you found her?"

Vince glared with loathing at his older brother, Anthony, slouched in the leather chair facing Vince's desk. He looked awful. Like he hadn't showered or shaved in weeks. His hair was too long and his clothes ratty. Vince struggled to understand how they'd come from the same gene pool. "Not yet. I can't believe your stupidity."

"How was I supposed to know she'd divorce you and take off? I mean, what did you do to her anyway?"

Vince curled his fingers into a fist. "Nothing."

"Something," Anthony shot back.

Ignoring the barb, Vince asked, "What did you tell Fernando?"

"What you told me to. He said he'd wait until New Year's Day. If we don't return the money, he'll kill us."

Vince spread his hand on the desk and leaned forward. "He can kill you with my blessing."

Anthony's dark eyes held malice. "Just remember what I did for you."

Vince swore and moved to the window.

They'd been teens, running with the other punks in the neighborhood, dealing dope, stealing what they could just for something to do. One night they'd knocked off a liquor store, but before they could get away, a cop showed up and caught Anthony. He'd gone to jail and never ratted on his baby brother.

Anthony never let Vince forget that if he'd had a rap sheet, he wouldn't have been admitted into law school.

But after twenty years, that card was wearing thin.

"I'll find her and get your money." Vince turned toward his brother. "And then we're even."

Anthony stood and walked to the door, his tennis shoes leaving smudged tracks in the cream-colored carpet. "Yeah, whatever you say."

After he left, Vince picked up the picture of his wife. "I will find you. And you will never leave me again."

Luke couldn't concentrate.

Every time he tried to focus on the paperwork lying on the desk, his mind conjured up the image of a cat-eyed blonde. Once again his curious nature wanted to know what was going on with Faith Delange.

He shouldn't be spending time thinking about Faith. There was still so much to do on the ranch. He'd lost two hands last week because they'd wanted to find a warmer place for the winter. His foreman,

Leo Scruggs, was having a hard time finding replacements. The roof on the house and one of the barns needed fixing and a llama would be birthing soon.

Ever since he'd returned to the ranch, his life hadn't been his own. Every day he found himself becoming more like his father. And the more he enjoyed being a rancher, the more scared he became.

This wasn't the life he'd wanted. He'd wanted excitement and adventure. At eighteen, he'd taken his desires to the Lord and had been steered toward the military. Knowing he'd had God's blessing, Luke had applied and been accepted at West Point. The years there were grueling, exciting and character building. He'd walked away with a degree in engineering. But the military still beckoned, even after his five-year service obligation.

Now, he held the rank of captain and his position of authority gave him more opportunity to make a difference in the lives of his men. From the beginning, he'd felt he'd been called to share his faith with his comrades, and now Luke was looked to as a source of comfort and hope.

He'd worked alongside the chaplain to form a Bible fellowship study, and he was constantly awed by the power of Jesus's love working in the men's lives. He didn't want to give that up.

He wished his father were still here.

Luke hadn't known about his father's cancer until nearly the end.

Your father is ill, the note had read, *come home.*

He'd arrived just in time to see his father before

he'd died. Guilt for not having been there ate away at him. If he'd only been a better son and kept in better touch. He'd have learned of the illness sooner and come home. He'd have been able to make his dad's final days easier.

And now, Luke was running his father's ranch and dragging his feet about leaving when all he really wanted was to get back to his own life, his unit stationed in the Middle East. He only had another twenty days of leave left.

He fired up the computer and looked up Faith on Google. A list of articles came up. Mostly charity events where Faith and her grandfather were present. One photo showed Faith in a gray business suit standing beside her grandfather who sat in a wheelchair. He was old and hunched with strong features. The caption read, "The Delanges to start a foundation for overseas missions through a local church."

Philanthropy, faith, family and money. What was she running from?

A soft knock sounded on the door.

"Come in."

The door opened and Faith stepped in. He clicked off the web page.

"I don't mean to bother you. But…well, your mother's asleep and I don't know what I should be doing."

Luke hadn't the foggiest what she should be doing now, either.

She smiled uncertainly.

Luke stood and moved around the desk. "I'll show you to your room."

Faith followed him. "I think this place is wonderful. So warm and cozy."

"My parents have lived here since they were married. I don't think Mom has bought anything new since."

Faith stopped at the bottom of the stairs. Her finger traced a carving in the banister.

"Did that when I was ten. Dad just about blew a gasket." He laughed slightly. "I can still remember how he lit into me, saying, 'If you want to carve your name into a piece of wood, there's a whole stack of firewood out back that you can carve up after you split it all.'"

"He sounds like he was a good father."

"Yeah. Yeah, he was. Strict, but always fair. Even when we didn't see eye to eye, I never questioned his love."

But his father had questioned his son's love. How many times had Luke turned his back on the advice and instruction his dad offered? Luke would give anything to have that time back, to show his dad how much he loved him.

"That's wonderful," she stated, wistfully.

"Did you question your parents' love?" he asked.

Sadness entered her gaze. "My parents were killed when I was eleven."

"That must have been tough. Who raised you?"

"My grandfather."

"The one that had a heart attack?"

She nodded. "He passed on almost two years ago."

"Have you been traveling since then?"

Her expression became guarded. Wary. "No."

She moved away from him to stand beside her suitcases where he'd left them in the entryway.

As she bent to pick them up, he said, "Here. Allow me."

Taking her bags in hand, he led her upstairs, entered the sewing room and breathed in the scent of gardenias, his mother's favorites, perfuming the air. A dried bouquet of the white blossoms sat atop the dresser. He made a mental note to order fresh ones.

"This is lovely." Faith walked in and surveyed the room. She gently brushed a hand along the black sewing machine resting on an old wooden table. "Your mother's, I assume."

"Yes, Mom loves to sew. She's made most of her own clothes for years." Luke could remember wanting her to go shopping like other mothers, but Dottie had always been a frugal woman who insisted her own creations were as good as those found in some overpriced dress shop.

"I like your mother. She's nice."

"Thanks. She likes you, too." Luke was thankful for that. It would make leaving that much easier.

Walking to the closet door, he put his hand on the knob. "Here's a closet. It's yours to use and you can clear out the drawers in the dresser."

"Thank you. You've been so kind."

He acknowledged her gratefulness with a nod. "My room's next door and the bath is across the hall."

Faith blinked and asked, "Where does Reva sleep?"

"She has her own house to go to." Thankfully.

"Besides caring for your mother, is there anything else I can do?"

"You can relax." He thought back to her strange behavior on the way to the ranch and his observation that she didn't want to be seen. "Maybe you should tell me what you're running from?"

Her eyes got big. "I'm…I don't know what you mean?"

"Faith, it was obvious you didn't want anyone to see you leave with me. Why?"

She looked at her hands. They were shaking. He took them in his, noticing how slender and vulnerable she felt. "Tell me this. Are you in trouble with the law?"

She lifted her head. "No."

He could see the truth in her gaze. "Okay. I'll stop pushing for now. But, Faith, if you need to talk, I'm here. You can trust me."

Faith nodded, her expression unreadable. "I'll go check on Dottie."

The second she left the room, Luke dropped his head on the doorjamb. Great. Now he was offering to be there for her when he knew he would be leaving soon. He shouldn't let himself get tangled up with her. As along as she posed no threat to his mother. He wasn't going to get involved.

He just had to stay strong, remember his goals, and not let himself get diverted from his path. Pushing away from the door, he headed out to visit the llamas and to let God know just how much he needed His strength.

* * *

After making sure Dottie was comfortably settled for the night, Faith went back to her room. She sat on the bed, elbows propped on her knees and her chin resting in her palm. The afternoon had flown by as she and Dottie talked. There hadn't been any sign of Luke, not until dinnertime. He'd come upstairs carrying two plates heaping with a delicious-smelling rice-and-chicken casserole, which she assumed Reva had cooked.

When Dottie had asked why he wasn't eating with them, Faith noticed he'd glanced at her before saying he was going to eat in his office while finishing up some work. She'd been able to eat very little of the meal.

Had she made him rethink hiring her? She hadn't meant to be so obvious in the car. But the fewer people who knew where she was the longer she'd be safe. And the longer she'd be able to stay.

She finished unpacking and was about to crawl into bed when she heard the creak of floorboards outside her door.

Old fears surged, her muscles tensed. Was someone coming for her? Would someone bust through the door?

No! She was safe. It was only Luke going to his room.

Ugh! She couldn't jump at every sound. She'd drive herself nuts for sure doing that.

When the house finally grew quiet and still, she turned off the light. As tired as she was, it would be

a long while before she could banish the awareness
of the cowboy down the hall.

Early morning sun streamed through the barn
windows, casting long, bright rays over the horses
and the stacks of hay. The smell of the animals mingled with the hay.

Luke rested his hands on the pitchfork. Every
morning he came out to the barn and fed the horses.
He could assign the job to one of the hands, but the
chore had been his when he was younger and somehow the task helped to relieve his grief over his father's passing. Hard physical labor helped get him
through the worst of the pain.

When he'd first arrived, his father had barely
been alive. If only he'd come home earlier, Luke
thought for the millionth time as he pitched hay into
the first stall. Those last few hours together hadn't
been enough time to say all the things Luke had
wanted to say. He hadn't told his father how much
he admired him or how grateful he was to have had
him as a father. Luke would always regret the years
apart. The years of silence.

Once the funeral was over, Luke had harnessed
his energies to the ranch. Luke started the re-fence
on the entire acreage, started repairs on the barn
and the corral. Chores that should have been taken
care of long ago.

His next project, he decided, would be the main
house. It needed a new roof and the porch could
stand some work. Staring at the structure through
the double doors of the barn, he pictured a swing on

the front porch. His mother would like that. Luke shook his head in wry amusement. He shouldn't be looking for more reasons to stay.

His unit needed him.

It was past time for him to wrap things up on the ranch so he could leave right after Christmas. He could hire out the work that needed to be done. And for sure hire some more hands to replace the two that had left. His foreman needed a vacation, as well.

The burden of responsibility made Luke's shoulders ache.

At least he'd done something right by hiring Faith. For the past three days she'd been a constant companion to his mother. When he left he would be assured that his mom would be in good hands.

He picked up more hay with the pitchfork just as Faith stepped out onto the porch into the sunshine. He took a deep breath and enjoyed the view, noticing the way winter sunlight danced off her golden hair, reminding him of Christmas lights. Bright and shining. Beautiful.

Her light wool coat, buttoned to the top, looked warm, but wouldn't hold up once it snowed again. She wrapped slender hands around a steaming mug and walked to the porch railing. Leaning her hips against the wood, she stared out at the scenery and sipped from the cup.

Luke knew what she was seeing; he'd stood in the exact spot too many times to count. From that vantage point, one could view the cattle grazing and the Three Sisters Mountains—Faith, Hope and Charity—rising majestically in the distance.

Studying Faith's profile, he wondered, what's your story? A part of him wanted to delve deep and find out what she was hiding from. But he'd already decided he wasn't going to get any more deeply involved.

Faith turned her head toward the barn and Luke knew the exact moment she saw him. Her eyes crinkled at the corners and her generous mouth curved upward into a stunning smile. His pulse quickened. For a heartbeat, Luke almost convinced himself she was glad to see him.

Feeling like a schoolboy caught staring at his teacher, he raised his hand in greeting, and sucked in his breath when she sat the mug down and pushed away from the railing. Mesmerized, he watched her walk across the porch and down the stairs, every movement flowing from her with graceful ease.

From around the corner of the house Brandy bounded up to Faith, who bent to nuzzle the dog's neck. A ridiculous sense of jealousy tore through Luke. He rolled his eyes. *You can't be jealous of your dog.* But he would've given anything to be on the receiving end of Faith's affection.

Faith and Brandy came forward and stopped steps from where he stood.

Luke tipped his hat. "Morning." Up close, she was even more attractive.

"Good morning, Luke."

He tore his gaze away from hers with effort and stared down at Brandy. "Seems you found yourself a friend."

Her hand stroked behind the dog's ears. "Yes, I have."

"It's good to have friends," Luke remarked, once again plagued by questions about this woman.

"Uh-huh."

The noncommittal answer made him frown. "Did you leave many friends behind?" he asked.

Visibly tensing at his words, she clasped her hands together, the knuckles turning white. "Some." The single word echoed in the barn.

"It's hard leaving behind the people you love." He said it more as a statement than a question, knowing firsthand how hard it was to walk away from the important people in his own life. And how difficult it would be to do again.

"Yes, it is," she agreed softly.

"Do you want to talk about it?"

She shook her head, her expression wary.

"I'm a good listener." What was he doing? He'd told himself he wasn't going to do this.

She gave him a tentative smile. "Thanks, I'll remember that. Actually, I was hoping you'd help me get your mother downstairs when you have a chance. She's been walking around upstairs but she'll need help negotiating a flight of stairs. The first time we try, I feel you should be present."

"Sure. When I finish here I'll be right up."

"Great. Dottie will be so pleas—" She stopped and cocked her head to one side.

The crunch of gravel sounded on the drive. But from where they stood they couldn't see the vehicle.

"Are—are you expecting someone?" Faith's voice changed.

Luke heard and saw the fear sweeping over her. "No, but people—friends—stop by all the time."

The vehicle on the drive stopped and the sound of a door opening and closing echoed in the chilly air.

In one swift, graceful motion, Faith darted to a darkened corner of the barn where she pressed her back against the wall, her hands fisted at her sides.

"Faith, you're safe here—" Luke was silenced by the finger she put to her lips and the look of terror on her face.

"Okay, God, please cover me," Luke mumbled and moved closer, positioning himself between Faith and the door. A brief look of comprehension passed across her features before they heard the heavy footfalls coming toward the barn. Each step drew the unknown closer.

Luke tensed in response to Faith's palpable apprehension. But how could he protect her when he didn't know what she was afraid of?

A small, panic-born whimper escaped her as a man stepped into view.

FOUR

Luke exhaled a rush of adrenaline and moved forward. "Matt Turner, you old dog."

As he shook Matt's hand, Luke glanced at Faith. The tension in her expression eased and her body went limp against the barn wall.

He figured Faith could use a moment alone.

Guiding Matt toward the empty corral, Luke stationed himself so he could see the barn. "What brings you out this way so early?"

Matt pushed back his black cowboy hat. "Just thought I'd come and see what my good buddy's been up to. We haven't seen much of you since you came home. Sally'd love for you to come out to the house for dinner some night."

Luke smiled at the invitation and the note of affection in Matt's voice for his wife. The couple had been high school sweethearts, clearly meant for each other. Luke and Matt had been friends since they were in diapers, and Luke should have made an effort to see the couple and their kids.

"Dinner would be great. I'd like that." Luke kept his eyes on the barn. Was Faith okay?

Faith stepped from the shadows and looked in his direction before hurrying toward the house.

What was going on? He wanted to know what had her so tied up in knots. He wanted to protect her. Help her.

But first, he had to win her trust.

Inside, Faith struggled to calm her racing heart. The panic still hadn't abated, but at least she could take a breath now. Dottie chatted away, oblivious to Faith's inner chaos. And Faith couldn't track the stream of words. She wanted to be attentive. She really did.

But her focus, her self-preservation instincts demanded her attention. She stared out the window at Luke and his friend.

How could she explain to Luke about the overwhelming sense of danger she lived with?

If she told him why she was running, what then? Would he ask her to leave? Or would he want to play the hero and promise to protect her?

She gave a silent scoff. No one could protect her. Hadn't she already learned that lesson well enough?

Maybe she should leave now, before she became too attached to Dottie, Luke and ranch life.

The thought of leaving brought sadness to her heart. She wanted to stay and make sure Dottie fully recovered.

Luke's confidence and trust in her judgment about his mother's care had warmed her. It'd been so long since she'd felt anything but the icy chill of fear, she'd forgotten how nice it was to feel heated from the inside out.

"Faith," Dottie said, concern evident in her voice. "Honey, are you all right?"

Turning toward the woman propped up against the pillows on the bed, she said, "Yes. Yes, I'm fine."

She would be fine here on the ranch. Here she was safe. Her paranoia had gotten the better of her earlier. She'd have to be more careful not to let her fear show.

Putting the episode behind her, Faith sat on the edge of the bed and made a conscious effort to concentrate as Dottie explained the basics of knitting.

As Faith cleared the dishes from dinner in Dottie's room, Dottie touched Faith's hand and gave a gentle squeeze. "Thank you, my dear. You are an answer to my prayers. You can't know how grateful I am that you're here."

Impulsively, Faith bent and kissed the older woman's cheek. More than Dottie could know or Faith could explain, being at the Circle C was like living another life. A life infinitely better than her own. "And being here is an answer to *my* prayers."

She was determined not to allow any more bouts of paranoia intrude on her peace of mind.

"Faith, why do you seem so sad at times?"

"I'm tired." That didn't answer what she'd been asked, but it was the best she could do. She tried to smile past the sudden tightness of her rib cage.

Concern marred Dottie's brow. "It's more than

that." Her eyes narrowed shrewdly. "Faith, I'm here if you want to talk."

The knot tightened at the offer of a confidante. How she wished she had the fortitude to spill her secrets to this kind woman, but Faith wouldn't risk the Campbells' safety any more than she had to.

Her throat constricted, making speech difficult. "I appreciate your concern, Dottie. I'm—I'm really just a little worn out." Worn out in many ways.

Doubt clouded Dottie's eyes. "You're probably hungry, as well. You hardly touched your food again at dinner. Why don't you go down and fix yourself something to eat before you go to bed."

The thought of food made her stomach roll. Admittedly, the little she'd eaten had been very good. She made a mental note to compliment Reva. "I'll be fine. It's hard adjusting to new surroundings."

"You really should eat more. You're too thin."

Faith smiled at the familiar words. Her grandfather had often lamented that she would blow away in a strong wind. "I'll eat a big breakfast."

Dottie nodded.

Faith helped Dottie settle back against the pillows. "Can I get you anything?"

"No, dear. Thank you."

"Then I'll let you get some rest." She turned to go.

"Faith?"

"Yes?"

"God is a great listener. He longs for His children to give Him their burdens."

Faith blinked. "His children?"

Dottie nodded. "He looks at all of us as His children. And as any parent wants to do, He wants to comfort and protect. That's not to say He'll rescue us from all our troubles, but He promises to be with us, offering wisdom and guidance."

The thought of God as a benevolent and loving parent boggled Faith's mind and opposed everything she'd been taught.

Hadn't grandfather often claimed that God sat in judgment of each individual and that His righteous wrath would fall upon the heads of those who opposed Him?

A dull ache started at her temple. Was what Dottie said fact or fiction? How did she go about finding the truth? Faith rubbed her eyes.

"Oh, honey, I'm sorry. Here I am yapping away when you need your rest."

"That's okay, Dottie." Faith managed to smile. "I'll see you in the morning."

Quickly, she left the room.

In the dimly lit hallway, a hand touched Faith's arm. She gasped. Her heart slammed against her chest. She jerked back. And focused on Luke.

She sagged against the wall. The sudden fear went spiraling through her abdomen where it landed in her stomach with a burning crash. "You scared me."

"Sorry, didn't mean to." He had the grace to look sheepish. "We need to talk."

A heaviness swept over her, weighing her down. The urge to run and hide streaked through her, but she couldn't make her feet move. Deep inside she knew her only real option was to stay and face his curiosity. But did it have to be right now?

"Can't this wait until morning?" she asked.

"No, we need to discuss what happened in the barn and what, exactly, you're running from."

The tightness in her chest spread, and her breathing turned shallow. *I'm running from the outside world,* her mind screamed.

The mere thought of what waited for her out there made her head spin and lights explode in her vision.

"Faith, what's wrong?"

She heard his voice, heard the concern in his tone. The words echoed inside her head, making the already dull ache grow and sharpen. She really should have eaten more.

Between her low blood sugar, the unexpected fright of moments ago and Luke's probing, Faith was helpless against the inevitable.

She tried to answer, her mouth opened, but no words formed. The hall grew dim and her vision closed in upon itself while the world faded away.

She heard Luke anxiously call her name.

Luke caught Faith before she crumpled into a heap at his feet. He checked her pulse. The beat steady. The slow rise and fall of her chest showed she was breathing.

"Faith? Faith. Honey, wake up." Patting her cheeks didn't seem to help any.

Scooping one arm beneath Faith's legs and the other under her back, he lifted her. She was soft and light in his arms as he carried her to her room. A faint, pleasing smell of flowers scented her hair.

Trying not to jostle her much, Luke laid her on the bed then sat on the edge and rubbed her hands.

She stirred, her eyelids fluttered, then slowly opened.

Unexpected tenderness grabbed a hold of him. He tucked a lock of blond hair behind her ear, his fingers brushed across her cheek, the skin satin smooth and warm to his touch. Her eyes widened slightly and he withdrew his hand. "How are you feeling?"

"Wh—what happened?"

"You fainted."

Her teeth pulled at her bottom lip. "I guess I'm more tired than I thought." She smiled, weakly.

It was from more than fatigue.

He studied her face, liking the way her dark blond brows arched high over eyes that slanted ever so slightly upward at the corners, the way her little nose wrinkled up when she didn't like something, and especially the shape of her mouth.

Full and lush. Kissable.

Faith sat up, her body barely inches from his. "Luke?"

Her voice held a question or an invitation, he didn't know which.

He swallowed but made no move.

She was beautiful and sensitive, strong and yet, so vulnerable. She was defenseless, exhausted, and in need of his protection, not his kisses. Plus, this was exactly what he'd been trying to avoid.

He didn't want an entanglement.

He jumped to his feet. One second longer and his

resolve would have weakened. A man could only withstand so much.

"I'll—I'll just let—you get some sleep," he stammered and tried to back out of the room gracefully, but bumped against the doorjamb. "I'll—see you in the morning." He exited quickly, pulling the door closed behind him.

Smooth, Campbell. Real smooth.

Disgusted with herself, Faith flopped back onto the pillows. What was the matter with her? She'd never felt like this before. And the last thing she needed was to kiss Luke. Yet, she'd wanted to.

More than she could have ever imagined.

Uh-oh.

She must fight this attraction to him. He was her employer. She couldn't allow him to turn into anything more. Not only would her job be on the line, but her safety.

And Dottie.

Faith wouldn't want to be forced to leave her if something went…wrong.

Though her mind agreed, the rapid beat of her heart contradicted the logic.

She couldn't let her heart rule. Not in this situation.

Too much was at stake.

Morning found Luke sitting at his desk, staring out the window. The Three Sisters Mountains rose high in the distance, their snow-covered peaks creating a breathtaking view.

But the beauty of nature offered him no peace. He hadn't slept much the night before. His mind wandered during his nightly devotions. He'd finally shut his Bible and dropped to his knees. Praying had always been a time of restoration and peace, a way to calm his mind before going to sleep.

But sleep proved to be elusive.

Images of Faith, her mouth inches from his, had haunted his dreams. He'd gotten up early, intent on getting some work done. After giving his foreman, Leo, permission to go into town to hire some hands, Luke meant to take advantage of this dry cold spell and start calling some roofing companies to come out and give him a bid, but so far he'd only managed to drink a pot of coffee.

The jingle of the phone pulled his gaze from the mountains to the phone on his desk. Picking up the receiver, he heard voices coming over the line.

"What do you need, Ethel?" Reva asked impatiently, having answered the phone in the kitchen.

"Just tell Luke I'm on the phone." Ethel's annoyance was clear in her tone. Ever since Reva had made Ethel's daughter, Molly, cry at their high-school graduation, Ethel had little tolerance for the woman.

"He's busy working. I'll take a message," Reva insisted.

Luke spoke up. "I've got it, Reva. You can hang up."

"But, Luke, honey, you said you didn't want to be disturbed." The whiny quality of her voice grated across his already tightly strung nerves.

"It's okay, Reva, just hang up." He waited until he heard a click. "Sorry, Ethel. What can I do for you?"

"Well, I thought I'd better call. Some man came in this morning, nosing around about that gal you had breakfast with."

Luke sat up straight. "What did he want?"

"He flashed her picture around the diner and wanted to know where he could find her. Of course, half the folks in here today were in here the other day. Everyone agreed that the woman in the picture was the one who had talked with you. A few people said they saw her get in your rig before you left town."

The worry in Ethel's voice mirrored the anxiety gathering steam in his belly.

"Did the man say who he was or why he wanted to find her?" His muscles bunched in anticipation of the answer.

"Just said he was a private investigator. He's on his way out to your place now."

An anxious ripple cascaded over him. A private investigator. He mulled that over in his mind. "Thanks for calling and warning me, Ethel. I owe you."

"You be sure to take care of that pretty little gal. I have a feeling she's in some sort of trouble."

"I will. Thanks, Ethel."

Luke started to return the receiver but he hesitated, listening to the click from Ethel hanging up and then another audible click. Anger tightened the muscles in his jaw.

He walked into the hall and raised his voice, "Reva!"

She stepped into the doorway of the kitchen wearing a tight leather skirt and high boots. Her pink fuzzy sweater looked like sticky cotton candy. "Yes, dear?"

Holding on to his patience, he gritted his teeth. "Do not call me dear. And do not listen in on other people's conversations. It's rude."

She blinked. "I don't know what you're talking about."

"Yes, you do." He spun on his heels and went in search of Faith.

After checking upstairs, he went out the front door. He saw her standing at the fence, petting the llamas. Her blond hair hung loosely about her shoulders, swishing with every move of her head. She looked both out of place and yet perfectly at home in her wool coat and jeans.

Luke gave himself a shake. There was business to attend to. He wanted to be ready when the private investigator showed up, and for that, he needed to know what he was dealing with in order to protect everyone on the ranch. As Ethel said, the girl was in some kind of trouble and he refused to go into the situation blind.

He approached the fence and several llamas came to him wanting attention. He nuzzled each for a moment, aware that Faith had also turned toward him.

"Good morning."

Her tentative greeting charmed him. "Morning."

A smile curved her lush lips and reached her eyes,

making the kaleidoscope of colors sparkle. The sharp winter sunlight glinted off a thin silver chain around her neck. Luke noticed the tiny box lying against her skin.

He pulled his attention back to the animals. "That's Blondie."

"Excuse me?" Faith's expression filled with confusion.

He nodded his head toward the animal which had its nose nestled in her hair. "The llama."

"Oh." She leaned her head onto Blondie's neck. "She sure is friendly."

"Uh-huh." Luke turned away. He frowned, aware that this wasn't the first time he'd felt deprived because she was giving her affection to one of his animals. He didn't like the feeling. He told himself he didn't want her affection.

She turned back toward the mountains. "Luke, about last night."

His stomach clenched. Last night, he'd made an idiot of himself. He'd shied away from her and their mutual attraction like a skittish colt.

But he wouldn't think about that right now. There were more pressing matters to discuss. "Faith, I need to ask you something."

"I know." She sighed heavily. "You want to know about why I panicked in the barn. But, really—I—there's nothing to tell. I don't—I don't know why it happened. I suppose I've been traveling alone for too long."

"Faith, look at me."

Slowly she turned and their gazes locked. He saw

her unspoken plea to let it go. And he supposed if the situation hadn't taken on a new edge, he might have tried to accept her explanation. But, at any moment, a man would be driving up and they needed to be ready.

"Why would a private investigator be looking for you?"

Even though he expected a reaction, the change was dramatic. Her eyes widened, the color drained from her complexion and for a moment he thought she'd faint again.

In a sudden movement that sent the llamas stumbling back, she darted past him and ran toward the house. He was so startled by her action, it took a full thirty seconds before he was able to make his feet move.

FIVE

"No, oh no. Please, God, no. Oh, no."

Faith put a hand to her throat, her breath coming in short, shallow bursts. Her mind raced. If a private investigator had tracked her down this quickly, it was only a matter of time before Vince showed up. She couldn't be here when that happened.

What a fool she'd been to believe God cared. He would never provide her with sanctuary. She wasn't safe, not even on a ranch in the middle of nowhere. Vinnie's tentacles reached far and wide, and now she'd put good, decent people in jeopardy because she'd selfishly wanted to pretend to have a normal life.

Shame and dread vied for a place in her heart. She could hear the harshness of her breathing while she struggled to pull out her suitcases. After dumping them on the bed, she began stuffing the contents of the dresser drawers into the open bags. Haste made her sloppy, but she didn't care. She rushed to the closet and took the clothes, hangers and all, and stuffed them into the bags. The cases wouldn't close.

"Close. Come on, close," she muttered. Her hands shook so hard she couldn't hold on to the fasteners.

Luke appeared in the doorway. He stood with his arms held rigidly at his sides, his body tense. She could feel his gaze on her and guilt clawed at her insides, the pain only adding to her urgency. She'd put his family in danger. He'd never forgive her when he learned the truth.

The crunch of tires on the ice-crusted drive below her window filled the air, and panic seized her, its grip tight and strong. She turned her back on Luke and looked wildly around the room. She had to get out of there, but how?

She made choppy, shaky slashes in the air with her hands. "Okay, okay. Think. Think."

She couldn't think. Her brain was having a malfunction. Somewhere, deep inside, the thought that it was over came crashing through. "God, please not like this."

Luke's hands settled on her shoulders and turned her around. She tried to shrug away. "No, no. I have to get out of here." She struggled against the strength of his grip, but his hold only grew tighter.

"Shh… It's okay." He gathered her hands in his. "I'm not going to let anything happen to you."

His words rumbled through her offering solace.

What was she to do now? He said it would be okay, but it wouldn't. She was trapped.

Outside, Brandy barked wildly and a car door slammed shut.

Faith jumped.

"Let me handle this."

Luke's voice washed over her, the timbre throaty and deep. He stroked her hair, then her cheek, wiping away tears she hadn't realized she'd shed.

"What will you say?" she asked.

"I'll think of something," he said, his voice stronger now, authoritative, in command.

"But…" Would he be able to put off the P.I.? Either way, she had to leave. Once Luke learned the truth, he'd send her packing, anyway. He'd have to. To protect his family.

"Trust me, Faith."

She hesitated. Trust was given in two ways—one, by someone earning that trust, and two, by a leap of faith. At this moment Luke held her life in his hands and he wanted her to trust him. It was a combination of both that made her nod slowly.

"Later, you will tell me what's going on." His tone held a silent warning. He wouldn't be put off any longer. "Stay put and out of sight."

He gave a short nod of his head and then disappeared, his footsteps receding down the stairs and out the front door. Faith ran to the window and peeked out the corner of the curtain. Below, a short, balding man, looking very much out of place in his off-the-rack suit and tie, held out his hand as Luke came into view.

Sinking to the floor, she fingered the prayer box at her neck. "Oh, Lord, what do I do now?"

Tears once again welled up in her eyes and one by

one slipped down her cheeks. How was she going to find the words to tell Luke about Vinnie?

"What can I do for you, Mr.—" Luke's gaze raked over the man, noting the muscular build beneath the dark suit and red-striped tie. The hard lines etched into the guy's face put him at about fifty.

"Mr. Costello." The man held out his beefy hand.

Luke shook the offered limb. "What brings you to the Circle C, Mr. Costello?"

"I'm looking for a woman you might have seen."

Luke kept his expression carefully blank. "Oh?"

"Her name is Faith Palmero. Tall, blonde, cat-like eyes."

A sinking feeling anchored itself in Luke's gut. He frowned. "Palmero?"

"She's probably going by an alias." Withdrawing a photo from his inside pocket, he held it out. "Here, I have a picture of her."

Aware of the man's shrewd gaze, Luke took the snapshot and quietly sucked in his breath. There could be no mistaking the woman in the photo. Faith. The snapshot looked as if it was taken straight from the society pages.

A confident smile sparkled on her lips and her hair was piled high upon her head. Diamond earrings sparkled from her earlobes and a diamond and pearl choker accentuated the slender column of her neck.

Feeling sick, he handed the picture back. She didn't belong on a ranch in the middle of Oregon, so what was she doing here? *God, grant me wisdom now.*

"So, have you seen her?"

Snapping his mind to attention, Luke countered, "Why are you looking for her?"

"I'm sorry. Client confidentiality, you know." The man looked past Luke to the house. Luke turned to follow his gaze and saw Reva standing just inside the screen door.

Turning back around, Luke stifled the urge to grab the man by the collar. "Who's your client?"

Mr. Costello smiled tightly. "Sorry."

Luke fisted his hands. He wasn't going to let this man or anyone else harm Faith. "Is this woman in some kind of trouble?"

"So, you have seen her." Mr. Costello looked pleased with himself.

So much for his poker face. Luke shrugged noncommittally and hoped Reva would stay silent.

"People in town said they saw you with her." Mr. Costello's eyes narrowed.

"I met her the other day," Luke conceded. "Seemed like a real nice lady."

"Hmm. Did she happen to say where she was headed?" The man's eyes scrutinized Luke before he darted a glance at Reva, who blessedly stayed put.

"No, she didn't." Then inspiration hit. "Oh, wait. She did mention something about wanting to see the tundra."

If he wasn't going to get any information out of the P.I., he'd just as soon wish him on his way.

"Tundra?" Mr. Costello screwed up his face in puzzlement.

"Tundra, as in Alaska." That should keep him

busy for a while. Alaska was a big place and people there didn't tend to talk to strangers.

"You think she went to Alaska?" The man wrinkled his large nose in distaste.

Luke steered the man toward his rented car. "Yes, I definitely remember her mentioning Alaska."

Mr. Costello stopped. "Did she have a car?"

Luke shook his head as he opened the car door. "Not that I know of."

"Uh, well…thanks. If you hear from her, would you please give my office a call?" He handed Luke a card before sliding behind the wheel of the sedan.

Luke stepped back and closed the door. *When the tundra melts.*

The sedan slowly moved down the drive and out to the road. Luke looked down at the card in his hand with the man's name and a New York address. Crumpling the card, he turned toward the house.

Reva came down the stairs, purse in hand. "Who was that man?"

Maybe she hadn't heard their conversation. Luke didn't have time now to deal with her. "Nobody that concerns you."

Her mouth drew into a pout. "Oh."

Luke stood fast under her scrutiny and relaxed when she shrugged.

"I'm off to town for groceries."

Unease slithered down his spine. "Why now?"

"Well, I can't very well cook a soufflé without butter or eggs," she chirped and hurried to her sports car.

"Wait!" he called, not liking the timing.

She either didn't hear him or ignored him as she climbed inside. She sped away faster than she should. She'd let the subject go too easily. He should have stopped her just in case she had some idea of going after the P.I. and asking questions.

He could only pray she minded her own business.

Because right now, he had to talk to Faith.

"You can relax, he's gone." Luke's voice brought Faith's head up from where it rested on her knees.

"He's gone?" That seemed too easy.

Luke stepped farther into the room. "I told him you'd mentioned seeing the tundra."

Faith's heart melted to her toes. He'd protected her and without knowing why. "Thank you."

He saluted. "U.S. Army, ma'am. Specially trained to rescue damsels in distress or small countries from military aggression."

"It sounds like a well-rounded program."

"We aim to please." He moved closer and held out his hand.

Without hesitation, she placed her hand in his and allowed him to pull her to her feet. They stood toe to toe with her hand still encased within his grasp, the heat from the contact spreading over her like sunshine on frozen snow. She looked into his face and for one dizzying moment she thought he might kiss her. Standing so close to him made her ache with yearning. A yearning that overruled her head and tore at her heart.

"Who are you?" he asked, his eyes holding questions.

Alarm shot through her, effectively shattering the moment. She withdrew her hand. "No one you need to worry about."

He gave her a level look. "What is your last name?"

Tension, like a hard solid knot, twisted in her soul. "What does it matter?"

She knew it mattered a great deal.

He set his jaw in a stubborn line. "It matters, Faith."

Unable to meet his eyes, she stared at the scar on his jaw. Luke lifted her chin with the rough pad of his index finger until their gazes locked. "Tell me."

Pulling away from him, she walked to the window and stared out at the blue sky. How much should she say? Everything?

She closed her eyes tight. If she told him everything, he'd tell her to leave. Her fists clenched at her side. Leaving was the last thing she wanted to do.

She liked living on the ranch, she cared for Dottie a great deal and…her mind skidded away from examining her feelings for Luke. Suffice it to say, leaving would be more painful than anything else she'd had to endure.

But if the danger had moved on to Alaska, did she have to say anything?

With Vinnie's private investigator looking for her in the frozen north, she was safe on the Circle C. Why spoil it with tales of her sordid mistakes from the past?

"You know—how sometimes—you imagine

something and then when you're faced with the reality of it, it doesn't live up to the image in your mind?"

When Luke didn't respond, she turned to face him. The expression on his face showed his confusion but she also knew she had his attention. "Being here on your ranch, caring for your mother and—" Unready to finish the thought aloud, she dropped her eyes to the buttons on his shirt.

She took a deep breath and lifted her eyes to meet his gaze. "It has far surpassed anything my feeble mind could conjure up."

Luke's brows creased. "Faith…"

She held up a hand in a gesture of entreaty. "Please. I want the past to stay in the past. I just can't drag it all out for your inspection. It's not important."

"Faith, if you're in some kind of trouble with the law, you need to tell me."

"No. It's nothing like that. I haven't done anything wrong. I mean, it's just not important."

"You were scared out of your mind. You honestly expect me to believe it's not important?" He stepped closer, filling the space between them.

"It's not," she insisted and clasped her hands together to keep them from trembling. "You sent that man to Alaska. He won't be back and no one knows I'm here. No one needs to know I'm here. Please try to understand."

"I don't understand. Who do you *not* want to know you're here?"

He took her hands and held them tight. An anchor in the storm. The simple gesture weakened her already wobbly knees and tears welled in her eyes.

"It's a family matter, Luke. It has nothing to do with you." He was such a good man, he could never understand someone like Vinnie. "It just doesn't matter."

With the pad of his thumb he wiped away a stray tear coursing down her face. "It does matter. You matter, Faith."

The sincerity in his voice, in his eyes touched her deeply. If her heart weren't already in a puddle at his feet, it would've melted. She had to tell him the truth. Or at least a watered down version. "When my grandfather died, I came into a great deal of money. Money that other people thought they had a right to. The pressure just became too much for me. Now, those people are trying to bring me back."

"Who are these people?"

"Investors. Charitable organizations. People my grandfather promised money to but didn't include in his will. They have no legal standing, but it doesn't stop them from making my life miserable."

"You didn't want to give them the money?"

She hated the look of disapproval in his eyes. "It wasn't that. The situation was very complicated and overwhelming. No one had proof that grandfather had made any promises. I didn't know who to believe."

He took a deep breath and she held hers, waiting to see if he'd decide to let her stay or to send her on her way.

"Who's Palmero?"

There was no way to avoid telling him. "My ex-husband."

His jaw tightened. "I see."

"Are you going to make me leave?"

"Of course not," he replied. "You're welcome to stay as long as you want. You'll be safe here." He turned to go.

She had to know or it would eat her alive. "Luke?"

He turned back toward her, his gaze intense and focused. "Yes?"

"Why—why did you protect me?"

"I like you," he stated simply.

"Oh." She hadn't expected the admission but it filled her with joy. Tears gathered at the back of her eyes again.

Luke tipped his hat and strode from the room.

Softly, she whispered, "I like you, too."

What kind of idiot am I? Luke tightened the stir-rup strap with a hard yank, drawing a snort from his horse, Winter.

"Sorry, boy," Luke muttered to the big, black beast.

It's a family matter.

My ex-husband.

The idea of Faith being married made something inside Luke cringe and grow hot. A curious burning sparked low in his abdomen and slowly worked its way up into his chest. He dropped his head to Winter's neck.

I'm struggling here, God. Really struggling. I need to stay focused on what I want. On what You want for me.

An image of Faith, her tear-filled eyes looking

at him so defenselessly slammed into his mind. His heart ached. Resolutely, he pushed her from his mind.

My career, Lord. That's what I should be focused on. I want to get back to my life, my ministry. The men need me.

More images of Faith barged into his consciousness.

The first time he'd laid eyes on her, standing in the doorway of the diner, her expression wary. Haunted.

Faith nuzzling a llama. The soft smile curving her lips. The look of contentment in her eyes.

The panic when he'd told her about the P.I.

The way her eyes had widened when he'd admitted he liked her.

Frustration ripped through him, leaving an aching wound in its wake. Muttering, he shook his head. "Cut it out. You're leaving and she has no place in your life."

A verse of scripture came to him. Luke closed his eyes. "Bear one another's burdens, and thus fulfill the law of Christ."

He'd been trying to live that verse through his work in the military. Now he was to take on Faith's burden, too?

He couldn't turn his back on her.

Not like he'd done with his father. His chest squeezed tight. If he'd cared more for his parents than himself and his career, maybe his father wouldn't have gotten so sick. And his mother wouldn't have had a heart attack.

His shoulders weighted down with guilt and remorse for his selfishness, he led Winter out of the stall. He needed to ride and clear his thoughts, but as he mounted Winter he glanced up and saw Faith at the window.

Her image was forever branded in his mind.

Faith went to the window in Dottie's room, again. She scanned the distance for any sign of Luke. It'd been hours since she'd seen him gallop off, kicking up mud and snow. She hoped he wasn't angry with her, or worse, disappointed. His opinion mattered to her. Though why, didn't make sense.

"Is something the matter, Faith?" Dottie asked, pausing in her daily routine of walking around the upstairs to get some exercise.

The late afternoon sun danced on the glistening snow. "Oh, no. I was just thinking how beautiful it is outside."

"It is nice out. I think we should go out and enjoy what's left of the afternoon while we can." An eager smile lit Dottie's features, making her appear healthy and younger than her fifty-eight years. "I heard the weatherman say we'd be seeing more snowfall within a few days."

"Then let's enjoy today while it's clear."

"Sounds good to me. Shall we go outside?"

"Let's."

It might even help take her mind off her troubles.

Taking Dottie by the arm, Faith helped her down the stairs. After the first venture outdoors with Luke's help, Faith had managed to help Dottie herself, thanks to Dottie's returning strength.

They could hear Reva in the kitchen and by silent

agreement they went out the front door. As they went down the porch stairs, Faith scanned the road in the distance. A pickup truck carrying bales of hay went by. On the left side of the drive, beyond the fence, the llamas stood in small groups, grazing on scattered hay. The corral on the right side of the drive stood empty.

"I love days like this." Dottie turned her face up to the sun. "Blake used to say the clean, fresh winter air made the move to Oregon worthwhile."

"You didn't always live here?"

"Oh, no. Blake and I were originally from Salt Water, Texas. We moved here right after we got married." Dottie started down the drive toward the llamas. The snow had been shoveled off to the sides to form small mounds.

Faith fell into step with her. "Do you still have family in Texas?"

"We do. Both Blake and I have siblings still living there. Sometimes I miss not having family close by and I think Luke missed out, too." Regret crept into Dottie's voice. "We weren't able to have any more children."

"I'm sorry."

"Oh, don't be. God blessed us with Luke, and Blake, bless his heart, thought of Reva as a daughter."

"And—you didn't?"

"No. No, we never really connected. Not even when she was little." Dottie sighed. "Her family lived on the next ranch over. She was always coming around, getting into things. Especially after her mama ran off. Then things went from bad to worse. Her dad drank himself to death."

"No wonder she turned to you and Blake."

Dottie nodded. "That she did. And Blake had always hoped that one day Luke would stop thinking of Reva as a nuisance and marry her."

Surprised by that tidbit, Faith had a better understanding of why Reva viewed her as a threat.

Reaching to nuzzle the first llama to reach them, Dottie cooed, "Ah, here are my beauties."

"Hi there, Blondie." Faith stroked the neck of a light-colored llama that had nudged her shoulder.

Dottie laughed. "That's Ricky. Blondie is over by the barn."

"Oops, sorry boy."

"You know, someday, I hope I'll have some grandbabies to spoil." Dottie gave Faith a sidelong glance over Ricky's head.

Faith stared ahead, choosing not to interpret Dottie's look. Instead, she fought down a sudden wave of jealousy for the woman Luke would someday marry and have children with. "You know there's only fifteen days left until Christmas."

Dottie's gaze clouded. "I'd forgotten. I usually have decorations up right after Thanskgiving, but—" Dottie sighed. "I haven't been in a very festive mood."

"That's understandable."

Taking Faith's arm, Dottie said, "But it's time to throw off the melancholy and get ready to celebrate the birth of Jesus. When Luke gets back he can get the decorations from the attic."

"That would be wonderful," Faith agreed.

This Christmas would be a celebration. She was free of Vinnie and with people she cared about.

What more could she ask for?

SIX

Luke stretched out his legs, his muscles tight from today's ride. He watched Faith sitting across the living room, her hands clenched tightly. She was still upset. The paleness of her skin concerned him. But she had no reason now to be afraid.

The private investigator was more than likely flying over the Canadian border by now.

For his part, the ride this afternoon had done nothing to dispel his frustration, because his thoughts had centered on Faith, alternating between the trouble she was hiding from and his growing attraction to her.

"Did you enjoy your dinner, Luke?" Reva leaned her hip on the arm of the chair he sat in. Something about the way she'd been overly sweet this evening set off warning signals in his brain.

He gave her a considering look. "Yes, you did a fine job, as usual."

With a satisfied smile, Reva walked back into the kitchen.

Hoping to catch a moment alone with Faith so

they could talk, he asked, "Are you heading upstairs, Mother?"

"No, actually. I'm feeling very perky this evening," Dottie said.

Faith glanced up with a wan smile and rose. "If you don't mind, I'll go to my room now."

Concern arched through Luke. "Do you need anything?"

"No, thank you. You both have been more than kind," she stated and went upstairs.

Luke debated following her. He really wanted to know more, but decided he had to let it go. He couldn't get too involved. "Can I get you some tea, Mom?"

Settling back in the cushy chair, Dottie patted his arm. "No, I'm good." She picked up the remote. "I'll just catch up on the news."

"I'm going to check on Lucy. I'll be back in a few." He turned to go.

"Luke?"

He stopped. "Yes, Mom?"

"Tomorrow would you bring in the Christmas decorations from the attic?"

His heart squeezed tight. Christmas without his father here was going to be tough. "Are you sure?"

Though her eyes misted, she nodded.

"Then of course."

"I think it will be good for Faith and I to decorate. Take her mind off whatever troubles her."

Family business. "I'm sure she'd like that."

"I like her," Dottie stated.

"Me, too, Mom."

A sage smile lifted the corners of Dottie's mouth. "Good. Now off with you."

"Okay, Mom." He hoped she wasn't getting any ideas about matchmaking. The last thing he needed was to have to be on guard from his mother's machinations.

When he walked into the kitchen, Reva was washing dishes. Now was a prime opportunity to talk to her. He leaned against the counter. "Tell me you didn't talk to the P.I. when you went to town."

Her hands stilled for a moment. She turned to face him and arched a dark blonde eyebrow. "Are you talking about the man that was here earlier?" Her mouth twisted sarcastically. "I didn't listen to your conversation."

He couldn't tell if she was telling the truth or not. "Thank you," he replied.

A gleam entered her eyes. "Interesting though that a private investigator would come to the Circle C. What did he want?"

"Nothing to do with you. And let's keep it that way."

Her mouth smiled but her eyes turned hard like slate. "Whatever you say, Luke. I only want to make you happy."

He frowned, not liking that statement. "You don't have to try to make me happy. That's not your job."

Inclining her head, she said, "I misspoke. I only want to be of help."

"We appreciate your help and we pay you well for it," he stated to clarify where their relationship stood.

"I'd want to be here even if you didn't pay me," she stated, her gaze softening, beseeching.

Uncomfortable, he headed to the door. "Good night."

He didn't trust Reva not to go snooping now that he'd piqued her curiosity. Tomorrow, he decided, he'd go into town and make sure the P.I. wasn't still hanging around.

"Costello found her."

Bob Grady's triumphant tone over the phone did little to appease Vince Palmero. "Where?"

"On a ranch in Sisters, Oregon. The guy that owns the place says she went to Alaska, but she's there."

"What's the guy's name," Vince snarled.

"Luke Campbell. Do you want us to grab her?"

"Not from the ranch. That would draw too much attention. Whatever you do, don't let her ditch you again."

"We won't. I've got a plan."

"Good. We'll talk again." Vince hung up and stared out the window of his fortieth-floor office. The Manhattan skyline was shrouded in shades of gray that matched his mood. Time was running out. His fingers curled into tight fists.

He had to get his wife back or he'd lose everything.

Faith toyed with her red cloth napkin, feeling unsettled and insecure in the Turners' home.

Get a grip and enjoy the evening. She forced her hands still. The Turners were very gracious people and their small house was decorated with festive red bows and green sprigs of pine that grew in abundance in this area. Tea lights flicked from the center of the table and reflected in the gold-rimmed dishes full of savory foods that scented the air.

The cozy setting and friendly atmosphere was foreign to her. In her grandparents' home, dinners were formal or taken in her room. Christmas decorations were a form of art, not something taken from outside.

With Vinnie, Christmas had been a lonely time. His family gatherings had been loud and chaotic but for Faith, she'd always sat on the sideline, wishing for some type of connection.

The type she'd found with the Campbells.

Though a week passed without incident, no more P.I.s, or anyone else showing up unannounced, Faith remained on edge.

She longed to go into town to explore the quaint old-west town decorated for the holidays. But she couldn't afford to be seen. She'd gotten good at coming up with excuses. Too good. And she hated always having to say no to Luke and his mother.

Even when it came to attending Sunday service.

But staying alone on the ranch with only Brandy as her protection had stretched her nerves taut and made her decide that this coming Sunday she'd risk being seen and go with them to church.

However, tonight Luke and Dottie had insisted she join them at the Turners' house for dinner and not wanting to be left alone, she'd agreed.

"A Christmas toast." Matt Turner raised his glass of sparkling cider high.

Faith picked up her glass. The light amber liquid sloshed around the bowl but thankfully didn't spill over the side.

"To a Merry Christmas. May we each find the blessing God has waiting for us." Matt's craggy face beamed at his wife.

"Hear, hear." Sally raised her glass in one hand while she held on to Jason, her two-year-old son, who sat on her lap shredding a paper napkin. White bits of paper fell to the floor at Sally's feet but she seemed oblivious to the mess.

Her dark eyes reflected the soft candlelight and her thick, brown hair had been pulled back into a braid that hung over one shoulder. Specks of paper stuck to her braid.

"What does 'hear, hear' mean, Mama?" six-year-old Gloria asked from her place at the table, next to Faith. In her little hand she held her plastic cup up high like the adults and her big brown eyes were wide with curiosity.

"It means I agree with Daddy," Sally replied.

"Why are we holding our cups up and what's toast got to do with it?" Gloria asked, her little nose wrinkled in puzzlement.

Luke's deep chuckle rumbled through Faith as their gazes met across the table.

Matt answered. "It's a tradition. You hold your glass high, say a toast, or a better phrase would be a blessing, and clink the glasses together."

"*Gently* clink the glasses together," Sally interjected.

Faith's gaze went from one Turner family member

to another. The love so obviously shared in this family overflowed, warming her heart. A lump formed in her throat. She ached with longing for a family of her own. Children to cherish, a husband to love. Maybe one day. One day when Vinnie was no longer tracking her.

"Dottie, will you be making pies again this year for the Christmas festival?" Sally asked as they all began to fill their plates.

Faith looked to Luke for an explanation.

"Every year the church has a big festival on Christmas Eve. The whole community gets involved."

"Maybe with Faith's help, I could make some pies," Dottie announced.

Luke raised his eyebrows at his mother.

"Of course I'll help," Faith said and ignored the voice inside her head that cautioned she might not still be here by Christmas. If that investigator found out that she hadn't gone to Alaska, he could come back to Sisters. And then she'd have no choice but to leave.

"That was so much fun," Dottie exclaimed as Luke drove home from the Turners'.

"It was. Thank you for insisting I tag along," Faith replied.

Luke smiled at her through the rearview mirror, glad to see the animation in her face. She'd been so nervous when they'd first arrived at the Turners'. But she'd quickly succumbed to the exuberance of the

Turner family. Luke was grateful for his old friends and their welcoming of Faith.

He turned the Bronco on to the driveway.

"Uh-oh," Dottie muttered. "Reva's here."

Luke pulled to a stop beside Reva's red car. He'd told her she didn't need to make dinner because they had other plans. Obviously she hadn't believed him. He helped his mother out of the car and preceded Faith and Dottie into the dark house.

"Reva?" he called out as he flipped on the lights.

She sat at the kitchen table. Luke recognized the hard light in her eyes and the grim set to her mouth. She was spoiling for a fight. He turned his attention to his mother and Faith. "Go on up."

Faith gave him a worried look before nodding slowly. His mother's mouth pressed into a tight line as she preceded Faith up the stairs.

As soon as they were out of sight, Luke turned to Reva. "Did I miscommunicate to you that we had plans tonight and wouldn't need you to come over?"

Reva crossed her arms over chest. "Where were you?"

Luke pulled out a chair and sat down. He held tight to his irritation. "Reva, don't you think it's time you started finding out what you want to do with your life?"

"I know what I want," she said, her gaze boring in to him.

Luke sighed. "You and I are never going to happen."

"Why not?" She reached out to put her hand over his. "I could make you happy."

He pulled his hand away. "Reva, don't do this."

Her expression crumbled, revealing the little girl that used to follow him around.

"But I love you, Luke."

He ran a hand over his face. He hated to hurt her, but he figured being brutally honest was the only way to get through to her. "I don't love you. Not like a man loves a woman he wants to marry."

She closed her eyes for a moment and when she opened them rage shone in the gray depths. "It's because of her, isn't it?"

He didn't have to guess who she meant. He had come to care for Faith, but her presence didn't change his feelings for Reva. "No. This has nothing to do with anyone but me. I don't love you. I never will. Now, I think it's time for you to go home."

Reva rose, and without another word, she stalked from the house.

Luke turned off the downstairs lights and then went upstairs. Faith was waiting for him in the hall. She still wore the black pants and white blouse she'd worn to dinner, but she'd released her blond hair from the rubber band that had held it back earlier. She looked so appealing in the muted light of the hall.

"She's pretty upset," she commented.

Her anxious expression pulled at Luke. "I know. Reva and I needed to have that talk. I should have done it a long time ago. I doubt she'll be back."

There was understanding in her eyes that made the harshness of what he'd done bearable.

"It's hard to say words that you know are going to hurt someone," she said.

"Yes. It is." He tucked a lock of hair behind her ear. "It's late. You should be in bed."

"I'm a little too keyed up to sleep, yet. I thought I'd make some tea. Would you care for some?"

He, too, was keyed up. "That would be great."

They headed back down to the kitchen. Faith put on the kettle and took two mugs from the cupboard. "Herbal?"

"Whatever you're having is fine."

She stuck a tea bag of his mother's favorite chamomile in each cup. They waited for the water to boil.

"Faith, tell me about your family."

Tilting her head to one side, she considered him for a moment. "What would you like to know?"

He wanted to know about her marriage. Did she still love her ex-husband? But he couldn't put voice to the question. Instead, he shrugged as she handed him a mug. "Start with your parents."

Taking a seat, she placed her steaming mug on the table and ran her finger over the rim. "My parents were—eccentric. Father loved to take pictures of everything he saw, and Mother loved to write about everything she saw. They made a good team. My grandparents thought their lifestyle was—well—that it was scandalous that they chose to spend their lives running around the world, sharing their experiences through pictures and articles. Grandfather wanted Father to take over for him. But Father would always say he had no head for business."

"Did they publish their work?"

"Oh, yes. In several of Grandfather's travel magazines. But they did it mostly for their own enjoyment."

"Your grandfather was a publisher?" She'd said a great deal of money, he just hadn't realized the scale she was talking about.

"Among other things. He always said media had the pulse of the nation. He'd started out with just a newspaper when he was a young man. He slowly worked his way to running half the newspapers, radio stations and television stations across the country."

"He was very powerful." And with that power came pressure. The pressure she was running from. He was beginning to get a clearer picture.

Faith nodded. "For a time."

"What happened?"

"Grandmother said that he slowly lost interest. His health began to slip and he didn't have Father's interest so he began selling his assets." She scoffed. "He was old school and didn't believe women could run multimillion-dollar corporations."

"So where did you fit in?"

She gave a small laugh. "When I was very small I went with my parents everywhere. I don't remember it too much, but I have impressions of exotic places that surface occasionally. About the time I turned eight, my grandparents demanded my parents bring me home for some schooling. My parents, bless their souls, believed I would get a better education staying with them, but since my grandparents funded most of their trips, they had to do as they were told. So I was sent off to private school."

"That must have been hard on you."

"I suppose. But Mother and Father came home often to visit. They would bring all sorts of odd souvenirs from the places they went. As I grew older, I went through a period of resenting them, but I grew out of that. I'm just glad they were able to live their lives the way they wanted."

The sadness in her voice made Luke's hand tighten around his cup. "It wasn't fair of your family to separate you from your parents."

Faith glanced at him then quickly looked away. "I suppose not."

"You said your parents died?"

She nodded. "A car accident. On my eleventh birthday, of all time. They—" Faith looked up at him with sad eyes. "They were on their way home to see me."

Setting his mug down, he reached over and covered her white knuckles with his hands. "I'm so sorry."

"It was a long time ago." She stared down at their clasped hands. In a low whisper Luke heard her say, "I never got to say goodbye."

Understanding her pain, Luke's heart ached for her. "When I heard my father was dying, I was afraid I wouldn't arrive home in time."

She lifted her head. "But you did."

"Yes, but there still wasn't enough time to tell him everything I wanted to say."

She nodded. "That's how I felt when my grandfather died." Tears rapidly filled her eyes. "I knew his death was coming but—I just wasn't ready." A tear spilled from her lashes and rolled down her cheek. "He'd had a heart attack five years earlier, after my grandmother passed on, that caused so much damage. He wouldn't have surgery and slowly he got worse until finally his heart stopped."

Luke stifled the urge to take her into his arms. He knew once he did he might never let go. "You were with him."

A small, sad smile touched her lips. "Yes. I was the only one he couldn't scare off. Grandfather was a prickly man on the outside but—I loved him a great deal."

"Tell me about him."

Faith moved restlessly, tucking and untucking her legs beneath her.

"Grandfather was—traditional."

"Like in women are women and men are men?"

"Exactly."

They shared a smile. "Did your grandfather believe in God?"

Her mouth twisted. "Oh, yes. He was definitely a God-fearing Christian."

"And he taught you to fear God," Luke stated gently.

"Yes, he did. He made sure that terror of God was deeply instilled." She quickly added, "But I knew Grandfather loved me. He just had a hard time showing his affection."

Luke ached for the little girl she'd been. Growing up without her parents, having her controlling grandfather warp her view of God. Faith deserved to be cherished and loved. "Fear of the Lord isn't about terror. It's about awe and respect. How can we love and obey a God we're terrified of?"

Her eyebrows drew together in puzzlement. "But isn't that why people obey God? Because they are afraid He'll strike them down if they don't?"

"God strikes down those who oppose Him, but not before giving them a chance to come to Him. And He always gives second chances. He gives humans free will to choose. Follow Him and receive all the blessings He freely gives or turn away from Him to live without the blessings."

She seemed to absorb his words, he wasn't sure she believed him. "Thank you."

He frowned. "For what?"

"For understanding. For giving me a job and a place to stay."

Her hazel eyes were direct, without guile. He liked that about her. "You're welcome."

For a moment silence stretched between them as their gazes remained focused on each other. Not awkward, but active. Two people finding something of interest in the other. Luke liked looking at her, seeing the beauty within her made his heart beat harder.

She slightly raised one eyebrow, bringing an end to the intimacy of the moment. "What made you join the military?"

He gave a mirthless laugh. "I didn't want to turn into my father."

A crease appeared between her eyebrows. "Why?"

Pride. He shrugged. "At eighteen, I guess I wanted a different, more adventurous life than my parents."

"And did you find that life?"

With a nod, he answered, "Yes. I started—"

Brandy raced into the kitchen barking wildly, the hair at her nape raised. She skidded to a stop at the back door, her nails scraping on the tile. Her barks deep and guttural, frantic.

Faith scrambled out of the chair. "There was someone at the window."

SEVEN

Heart pounding, Luke moved swiftly to the door and turned off the kitchen light, then turned on the outside porch light.

"Don't go out there," Faith pleaded.

His gaze searched the dark for the trespasser.

After a few moments, Brandy's barks tapered off and she paced, the fur on the back of her neck still raised.

Faith, her complexion pasty white, stood in the doorway of the kitchen, her body shaking. He went to her and took her hands. "Do you remember what the man looked like?"

"I don't know. I just saw a flash of movement."

"Could it have been Reva?"

Her brow furrowed. "I suppose. But why would she—?"

"She was angry when she left."

Faith looked unconvinced. "Should you call the police?"

"Luke?" Dottie called from the top of the stairs.

"Here, Mom." Luke moved into the entryway.

His mom stood on the landing, her robe hastily thrown on. "What's got Brandy in such a twitter?"

"Someone was outside," Luke replied.

"One of the hands? Is there a problem?"

"I don't know, Mom."

Faith touched his arm. "You go make your call. Dottie and I will be upstairs."

He could see fear lurking in her hazel gaze. "You're safe. I'm not going to let anything happen to you."

She nodded and ascended the stairs and led Dottie back to her room.

Luke called the sheriff's station. Thirty minutes later, Sheriff Bane and a young deputy arrived. After shaking hands with the sheriff and being introduced to Deputy Art Unger, Luke said, "Faith thought she saw someone at the kitchen window."

He told him about his conversation with Reva.

"Nothing like a woman scorned. Let's take a look." The sheriff grabbed a long, black-handled flashlight from his car and walked around the back of the house. The bright beam revealed footprints in the snow beneath the window. Sheriff Bane shifted his weight on to one leg and hovered his other foot over a clear print. "I'd say a size eleven or twelve boot. Too big for Reva. These are pretty deep, so I'd say a heavy man." He peered through the window. "Tall, too, to be able to see through this window."

The young deputy scribbled notes on a small pad.

Sheriff Bane swung the beam along the ground. "Prints disappear on the gravel drive. Who else is on the property?"

"My foreman and the hands live in the four apartments above the stables."

"Could it have been one of them?" the sheriff asked.

Shaking his head, Luke answered, "I don't think so. Brandy wouldn't have flipped out the way she did. Except—"

"Except?"

"I have two new hands, but Brandy knows them."

"Let's go see if they noticed anything or anyone lurking around," Sheriff Bane said. "Art, take a post outside."

Luke led the sheriff to the second-floor apartments in the bigger of the two barns. A light shone under the first door. At their knock, the door opened and Leo stood there in stocking feet. His frame was lean and lanky in jeans and a plaid shirt hanging open over a white T-shirt. His graying hair stuck up in tufts and his blue eyes regarded them sharply. "Hey, boss. What's up?"

"Can we come in?" Luke asked.

Leo stepped back and held the door wide. Though sparse on furniture—a refrigerator, stove, a small dining table and lone chair, a recliner and TV— the tiny space was cluttered with trophies, saddles, plaques on the walls and stacks of magazines and newspapers.

Luke had been nearly twelve when his dad had hired Leo. He could still remember being in awe of the cowboy who'd come to live on the ranch. Leo had been a rodeo star in his youth and he had stories that had kept a boy entertained for days on end.

"Mind telling me what this visit is about?" Leo asked.

Luke explained the situation.

"I ain't seen anyone around. I know the boys went to town tonight. Haven't heard them return." He shrugged. "That's not to say they haven't. I don't hear so well these days."

Luke hadn't thought about how Leo's health might be. Leo and his father hadn't been that far apart in age. Now, Luke felt a twinge of concern for his foreman. Maybe soon it would be time to talk to him about retiring.

The sheriff asked Leo questions about the other hands.

"Charles has been on the ranch for about three years now, ever since his wife left him. The two new guys came highly recommended by the Krofters, a couple of ranches over."

The sheriff took their names and then asked Leo to let Luke know if he saw anything out of the ordinary.

"Will do, Sheriff." Leo clapped Luke on the back. "Don't worry, boss. Nothing's gonna happen that I don't know about."

As they turned to leave, the sheriff paused. "What size boot do you wear?"

Luke opened his mouth to protest, but froze when Leo replied.

"An eleven."

No way would Luke believe Leo had been spying on them, and he said as much to the sheriff once the door closed.

"We can't rule out anyone," the sheriff replied as he moved down the hall to knock on the doors of the other three small apartments.

"Seems your hands are still out for the night. Do they do this often?"

Luke shrugged. "I don't keep tabs on their personal time. I'll talk to them tomorrow."

"Good enough." The sheriff and his deputy walked to their car. "I'll keep my eyes and ears open around town. And I'll have a talk with Reva." The sheriff opened the car door.

Relieved that he wouldn't have to deal with Reva himself, Luke replied, "That'd be great. Thanks."

He watched the car disappear down the drive before heading back inside.

"Did they find anyone?"

He came to a stop at the bottom of the stairs. Faith stood on the top landing. Her blond hair hung loosely over one of his mother's old terry robes tied securely at the waist.

He shook his head. "No. Whoever was out there is gone."

She stared at him a moment before inclining her head. "I'll see you in the morning."

"Good night," he said and watched her slip into her room. Then he grabbed a blanket from the hall closet and sat on the couch.

Brandy rose from her bed and nudged him with her nose before flopping down on the floor beside him. Within moments Brandy's soft snore was the only sound in the house.

Quiet enough to let Luke's mind wander to the beautiful blonde upstairs.

Reva May Scott hated country music. It was too depressing and too close to her life. But in a small town like Sisters, there wasn't any escaping the soulful ballads and honky-tonk tunes played on the jukebox in the corner of the Rib Eye Bar and Grill.

She sat on a stool at the long wooden counter in the bar area of the restaurant, feeling conspicuous as a single woman among so many couples out for a good time on a Friday night. She lifted her martini glass and took a sip. The sweet and sour concoction hit her taste buds with a snap. She didn't think the thing tasted that much like a Granny Smith apple, but the green color was sure pretty.

Especially on a dismal night like tonight.

It wasn't the weather bringing her down. In fact, she rather liked the dry air, snow-covered ground and biting temperature of winter in central Oregon. Much better than the drizzling rain on the west side of the state.

No, tonight was dismal for a different reason.

All she'd ever wanted was to be a part of a family. To belong to someone who would love, honor and cherish her. Just like all the marriage vows of all the people whose weddings she'd gone to over the years.

Silly words. Silly sentiment. Still, she wanted it.

She took another drink, letting the tangy liquid slide down her throat and the vodka take the edge off her hurt at Luke's rejection.

She'd had her heart set on Luke for so long she

couldn't remember when she didn't love him. Oh, he'd never professed any sort of romantic feelings for her, but she'd kept believing that in time he'd come around, just like his father had said. She'd hoped if she was close enough, did enough, then one day Luke would vow to love, honor and cherish her and she'd finally belong.

But not now. Not with Faith in the picture.

Anger burned in her belly, fueled by the alcohol.

That private detective should have hauled Faith off after Reva told him she was on the ranch and not on her way to Alaska.

But no. The creep had just smiled and left town.

Something had to be done. It just wasn't fair that this strange woman could come in and take Reva's place in Luke's life.

"Hey, beautiful, what are you doing sitting here all by your lonesome?"

Tensing at the unexpected intrusion, Reva slanted a glance toward the man who'd sidled up to the bar beside her. Recognizing him as one of the hands on the Campbell ranch, she relaxed. Not that she remembered the guy's name. He was new and not Luke. "Hey, yourself. Where are your buddies?"

"Oh, they'll be along. We each had stuff to do." He inclined his head toward her near-empty glass. "Can I buy you another?"

She wasn't stupid. A free drink was a free drink. "Why not?"

"Another for the lady and I'll take a beer," the man said as he sat on a stool.

"Thanks…uh. I'm sorry I don't remember your name."

His dark eyes danced with amusement. "That's okay. I remember yours. Reva."

She shrugged. His name wasn't important. He wasn't important. He wasn't Luke.

She picked up the fresh drink the bartender had placed in front of her.

"So what are we celebrating?"

Reva shook her head. "We're not."

"I didn't see you at the ranch today."

She snorted. "And you won't. Not while *she's* there."

He leaned closer. "You don't like the new lady?"

"No."

"You want her to disappear?"

Like a cloud of smoke. Poof. Gone. Reva giggled, the drink making her a bit woozy. "That'd be nice."

His voice dipped low. "I can help you with that."

"You can?" She leaned closer. "Tell me how."

Sunday morning roared in with a heavy dumping of new snow and a drop in temperature. After a quick breakfast of toast and coffee, Faith dressed for church and met the Campbells in the living room. Luke had on a tie with his cotton oxford shirt, jeans and cowboy boots. He looked like the perfect gentleman rancher.

He helped his mother into her long down parka over her wool dress. Her black sensible shoes and thick tights made Faith worry that she'd dressed inappropriately. Her own tennis shoes, khaki pants and striped turtleneck were as dressy as she had.

"Here you go," Luke said, now holding out the new parka he'd bought for her in town.

She slipped into the jacket, mindful of Luke's warm breath on her nape. "Thank you."

"Zip up. It's cold out there," he stated as he opened the door.

Faith shivered as much from the cold as from nerves about being seen in town as she slid into the back of the Bronco. Immediately, the fresh snow that had fallen on her head melted and dripped down her neck. Luke helped Dottie in before going around the front and hopping into the driver's seat.

"Now, let's hope the main road has been plowed," he said.

The Bronco eased forward down the drive, the tires crunching over gravel and ice. When they came to the main road, Luke stopped and let the vehicle idle. "Okay, ladies. The road is not plowed. I think we can make it, but we could get stuck."

That didn't sound appealing to Faith. Even with the heat on high, she was still cold.

Dottie sighed. "I'm not up to a walk in the snow if we do get stuck."

Faith met Luke's gaze in the rearview mirror. She wrinkled her nose. "Me, neither."

"All right then," Luke said and threw the Bronco into Reverse.

Once he parked the car back in front of the door, they all hurried back inside.

Luke immediately built a fire in the fireplace and

Faith went to set some water to boil for tea. Dottie sat in her recliner and covered up with a blanket.

Faith admitted to herself she was thankful she wasn't leaving the ranch. Once the water was ready, she brought out three steaming mugs and the basket with teas.

Dottie snagged a chamomile and Luke took a black tea. Faith dipped a spicy-smelling bag in her water.

"If you're up for it, Mother, I thought I'd invite the boys in for dinner tonight and give them their Christmas bonuses."

"That would be fine. Faith and I can create some gourmet meal. What do you think, Faith?"

"That would be wonderful," she replied, enjoying being included.

Luke set his mug down. "I'll go make sure the guys are all available. Though I don't imagine any of them will be leaving the ranch tonight."

Or anyone coming to the ranch, Faith silently added.

She could only hope the snow continued to keep the outside world from intruding.

"Wow, that was some meal," Jerry Ridgeway exclaimed, sitting back in the ranch's dining-room chair with a satisfied grin.

"You could say that again." Another ranch hand, Mac Stone, agreed while wiping at his mouth with a green cloth napkin.

"I'll say it," Charles Fry stated and rubbed at his gut in a satisfied gesture. "Fine meal."

Leo nodded his approval. "We have a keeper here, Dottie."

Dottie laughed. "Careful, Leo. You'll scare her off."

Luke glanced at Faith, who blushed under all the praise. She sat near his mother at the opposite end of the table. The festive Christmas decorations and delicious food foreshadowed the upcoming holiday. With Faith here, Christmas might not be as sad an occasion as Luke feared it would.

Faith seemed to have no idea of her effect on everyone in his house. The hands all seemed as smitten with her as his mother, who adored her. He didn't care to examine his own feelings for her.

Tonight they'd invited the hands to a pre-Christmas dinner so he could give them their Christmas bonuses. Even though Mac and Jerry were new, Luke had given them each a bit of extra cash.

Now, he pushed his chair away from the table. "That *was* a wonderful dinner, Faith."

"I'm glad you liked it. Your mother told me chicken and dumplings were your favorite." Her smile was tentative.

His mother beamed at him from her place at the head of the table.

Pleasure and unease seeped into his veins, heating the blood pounding through his suddenly racing heart. His mother definitely was trying her hand at matchmaking. "Thank you."

His gaze locked with Faith's. For a split second he forgot to breathe. In her eyes, he saw a myriad of emotions—yearning, wonder, and a hint of apprehension.

He wanted to explore the yearning and wonder, and rid her of any apprehension. But now was not the time.

For the past few days life had calmed down. No more Peeping Toms. Leo and the hands all promised to keep a vigilant eye out for any intruders. Reva hadn't shown up since his talk with her and the sheriff had called to say he'd questioned Reva about Friday night. Apparently, she had been in town at a bar the whole time.

Luke stood, breaking the eye contact with Faith and busied himself by gathering the empty plates.

Noticing her look of surprise, he gave her a self-conscious grin. "I'll help clean up, okay?"

"Uh, sure. That'll—be great." She pushed her chair back and stood.

Luke reached for an empty platter in the middle of the table just as Faith reached for it, too. Their hands brushed against each other and each let go as if burned by the same electrical current. The platter dropped noisily to the table and Luke jerked his gaze to Faith.

She slowly raised her gaze. "Slippery plate."

Laughter filled the room, relieving the tension. Luke chuckled and nodded. "Very."

Luke left the slippery plate to Faith and turned to carry his stack of dishes to the kitchen. He met his mother's mirthful gaze and knowing smile, and the significance of helping with the dishes suddenly struck Luke.

His father had helped his mother every night, claiming it was their time together. Luke had, on occasion, watched silently from the doorway as his parents worked side by side. Doing dishes had become an intimate act that he'd never wanted to intrude on. Anticipation catapulted his heart into triple time.

The rational part of his brain screamed a warning. He didn't want to get too comfortable in this domestic scene, but he was unable to resist.

His mother gracefully rose from the table, the twinkle in her eyes shining bright. Leo scrambled to pull out her chair.

"Thank you for dinner, Mrs. Campbell, Faith," Jerry said as he rose. "This sure beats microwave or restaurant food."

Mac and Charles rose as well, each adding their thanks.

"Any time, boys. We're glad to have you on the ranch," Dottie replied.

After the three men left, Dottie patted Leo's hand. "Would you like to join me for some tea?"

"Sure would," Leo answered.

Luke hesitated, not sure how he felt about his mother and Leo becoming chummy.

"I'll start some water," Faith offered.

Dottie gave her a grateful smile. "Thank you, dear."

She and Leo went into the living room.

Luke helped Faith clear the table while he wrestled with the thought of his mother socializing. It wasn't like she and Leo were going on a date or anything. Just two old friends having tea in the living room.

Get a grip. He wasn't his mother's keeper.

"You really don't have to help." Faith set the kettle on the stove to boil.

"Oh, but I want to." He picked up a dish towel. "You wash and I'll dry."

Faith arched a blond eyebrow. "And just why do I have to be the one to get dishpan hands?"

"You're the woman," he teased with a grin.

"Ah, that's rational thinking coming from a mere man." She rolled her eyes with an answering grin and turned on the faucet.

Within moments, steam rose from the hot spray of water.

"Here, I'll wash," Luke offered, realizing that as a society woman, she probably wasn't used to washing dishes.

She waved him off. "I was just kidding. I'll do it. It's not that big a deal. Besides, the chore is kind of soothing."

"Really?"

"Yes, really." She slipped her hands into the water and scrubbed a plate before handing it to Luke to dry.

A lock of hair fell forward into Faith's eyes and she blew at the stray wisp. Unable to resist, Luke reached out to brush back the strands and caressed her cheek. She turned to look at him, her gaze bright and trusting. He wanted to sink into her gaze, to taste her lips, to hold her close. His head dipped and gently he pressed his lips to hers, the contact sending jolts of sensation ricocheting through his system, making his toes curl inside his cowboy boots.

"Oh, don't mind me. I'll just grab a couple of cups and be out of your way in no time."

His mother's voice yanked Luke back to his senses. He straightened. Color rose high in Faith's cheeks. She quickly turned back toward the sink and plunged her hands into the water.

Luke leaned against the counter and took several steadying breaths.

"Would anyone else like some tea?" Dottie cheerfully asked.

"No, no thank you, Mother," Luke managed to answer, sounding somewhat normal.

"Well, you know, tea has a very calming effect."

Faith made a strangled sound and Luke stared at his mother through narrowed eyes. Dottie blinked at him. He glanced at Faith. Her cheeks turned bright red and her lips were pressed together in a tight line. She thrust a plate into his hands.

They continued in silence until Dottie left the room.

The second his mother was gone, Faith turned on him. "What was that all about?"

"What?" he asked innocently.

"You know perfectly well what." She stood with her soapy hands on her hips, sparks flying from her eyes.

"I'm sorry. It won't happen again."

Her mouth dropped open and then snapped shut. Abruptly, she turned back to the sink and Luke thought that was the end, but she whirled back around. "You're right it won't happen again, Luke Campbell. Next time you kiss me, you'd better mean it."

She threw a wet sponge at him, hitting him square in the chest, before marching out of the kitchen.

Luke stared at her retreating back in astonishment. Then a slow grin spread across his face as the implications of her words sunk in.

"Of all the insufferable, pigheaded, arrogant..." Faith punched her pillow, creating a nice round dent in the soft, downy feathers. The lingering effects of Luke's kiss coursed through her veins.

She groaned aloud and punched the pillow again. He'd had the gall to apologize. And say he wouldn't kiss her again. Faith buried her head beneath her pillow and willed herself to calm down. She really didn't want his kisses, so why was she so upset?

A soft knock startled her into a sitting position. Slowly, she got off the bed and walked to the door leading to the hall and paused with her hand on the knob. "Yes?" she whispered.

"Faith, we need to talk," Luke said.

"We can talk tomorrow."

The door wasn't locked but he wouldn't enter unless invited. Vinnie wouldn't have bothered to knock, he'd have just barged in. But she could trust Luke. He wouldn't hurt her. Especially, physically.

Any emotional hurt would be her own fault.

EIGHT

The next day, after his chores, Luke found his mother and Faith sitting in the living room, each with knitting needles and yarn in hand.

"Hello, ladies."

"Can I make you a sandwich?" Faith asked, her gaze somewhat shy as she rose.

"I can get it," he said and moved into the kitchen to wash up.

"I don't mind," she countered, her expression sincere as she followed him.

He relented. "That would be great, then."

Remembering how they'd parted last night made Luke's pulse quicken. He wanted to talk to her about the kiss and what it meant. Or didn't mean. Or what they wanted the kiss to mean. But with his mother watching he chose not to approach the subject now.

"Reva hasn't shown up again this morning," Dottie commented as she, too, entered the kitchen.

Luke turned his attention away from watching Faith make his sandwich and addressed his mother. "I don't know that she'll be back."

"Oh? Did something happen that I should know about?"

With a shrug, Luke replied, "I laid my feelings for her out on the table. She was pretty mad."

Dottie whistled. "Well. It had to be done."

"Here." Faith handed him a plate with a thick ham sandwich.

"Bring that in to the living room and talk with us," Dottie said.

Luke helped his mother to her favorite chair, and then sat next to Faith on the sofa, leaving mere inches between them.

Faith arched her eyebrows high and nodded to the rest of the sofa. "Is there something wrong with that end?"

He shrugged. "Not at all. Just more cozy here."

He liked the way she blushed. Her complexion turned a pretty shade of pink and her eyes sparkled. It wasn't nice to tease, but it was such fun.

Luke noticed his mother's interested stare and gave her an innocent look before taking a bite of his lunch.

"You behave yourself," Dottie admonished with a pleased smile.

"Always," he answered with a lopsided grin.

Faith snorted beneath her breath. He nudged her with his elbow. "What?"

She turned her face toward him and it took a great deal of effort not to lean in close and taste her lips. Instead, he gave her a slow smile and savored her blush.

His mother's voice drew his attention away from Faith. "I think I saw a raccoon this morning."

"They're seeking warmth. I'll make sure I let Leo know so he can plug any holes in the llamas' barn."

Dottie motioned toward the bookshelf against the wall. "Luke, hand me those photo albums, please."

"Ahh, Mom. You're not going to start showing my baby pictures are you?"

"But, of course." Dottie bestowed an innocent look on him. Faith burst out laughing.

Luke glowered in mock outrage. "You think that's funny, do you?"

Still laughing, she nodded.

"Well, I'll give you something to laugh about." He set his plate on the coffee table and then his hands found the tender spot on her rib cage and began tickling. She squirmed beneath the onslaught.

His mother's rich laughter stilled his hands.

Stunned, Luke couldn't ever remember being compelled to tickle anyone, let alone doing so in front of his mother. Embarrassed to his toes, he picked up his plate and stared at the big Douglas fir tree by the window. "The tree looks great by the way."

Mirth still danced brightly in Dottie's eyes. "Yes, it does. Thanks to Faith, the whole house is ready for Christmas. I can't believe just five more days. I need to go to town and do some shopping."

"I'll take you tomorrow, if you'd like," Luke offered.

"Perfect. Maybe we can talk Faith into coming as well," his mother said, her expectant gaze on Faith.

She swallowed and her expression showed the

panic going on inside her head. Luke had already assured her the P.I. had left town, so why was she still so worried? "Or we can pick up anything you need," he offered.

Her relieved smile didn't reach her eyes. "I'll make a list. The pharmacy has a refill that needs to be picked up."

"I can do that." He rose. "I need to check on Lucy."

"She's due soon, isn't she?" his mother asked.

"After Christmas."

"Lucy?" Faith asked.

"One of the llamas is about to be a mama," Luke explained as he retrieved the photo albums his mother had requested and handed them to Faith. "Have yourself a good laugh."

Faith took the offered books and looked up at him. Traces of panic still lingered in her gaze and Luke hesitated. Part of him wanted to gather her close and reassure her that everything would be all right. He wouldn't force her to go or do anything she didn't want to.

A bigger part of himself ordered him to stand down. He was getting too entangled. She was his employee! And that was a road he didn't want to travel. He forced himself to look away and breathe deeply.

After kissing his mother's cheek, he headed toward the door. On the threshold, he paused and looked back. Faith still watched him, her expression tinged by a sadness he didn't understand. He ached for her and felt a compelling pull to do whatever it took to make her relax.

Employee or not.

* * *

"And this picture was taken at Luke's sixth birthday party."

Faith stared at the snapshot of Luke wearing a miniature cowboy hat, leather chaps and showing a gap-tooth smile for the camera. Her fingertips brushed over the image.

Today she'd seen a glimpse of the little boy he must have been and she liked the playful side he'd displayed. She didn't know what to make of him. He'd protected her, kissed her and now teased her outrageously. He made her head spin so fast she became dizzy any time she tried to hold on to an emotion or thought.

She tried to analyze what she was feeling. She was attracted to Luke, there was no denying that. In her eyes he was everything a man should be, handsome, but not too pretty, gentle, yet with a quiet strength that made her feel protected. He'd been sensitive to her feelings so many times. He'd earned her trust.

But she couldn't allow herself to fall for him. He was a port in the storm of her life. And one day Dottie wouldn't need her any longer and Luke would return to his military career. And she'd…

She pushed aside her confusion and concentrated on the photo album.

"This is my Blake." Dottie pointed to a picture of a handsome man holding a small infant.

The resemblance between Luke and his father was uncanny. Faith touched the image. "You must miss him a great deal."

"Yes, I do. He was a good husband and father. Luke is a lot like him."

Faith smiled to hear the subtle suggestion in Dottie's voice. She didn't have to work too hard to know Dottie wanted her son to settle down and start a family. It's what every mother wanted for her children. Faith had no doubt he'd make a fine husband and father.

"Luke was an adorable child."

"That he was. He was also headstrong and willful." Dottie chuckled. "I can't wait for the day when he has his own kids and I can sit back to watch the fun."

She could picture Luke holding an infant, his strong, gentle hands cradling the tiny body. "Luke will make a good father."

"Do you like children, Faith?" Dottie's steady gaze pinned her to the sofa.

"Yes, but…I don't have a lot of experience with them." Almost none. Vinnie had refused to start a family, and now she was very thankful. Adding a child to the situation would have been so unfair to the child. But in the future? She dared not even dream that far ahead.

"Do you like my son?"

Dottie's blunt question startled her. "Uh, yes. I do like Luke. He's a decent man." Not to mention caring, sensitive and attractive.

"I think he likes you, too." Dottie's wistful expression made Faith's heart pound.

"He's a good employer," Faith said, hoping that

would put their relationship in perspective, for both her and Dottie.

Dottie's slight smile told her she wasn't convinced.

"What are you two doing?" Reva hovered just inside the doorway from the kitchen, a bucket of cleaning supplies in her hand. The tight pink sweater she wore optimized her cleavage.

Surprised to see Reva and thankful for the distraction, Faith answered, "Looking at some old photos." She hesitated a moment, sympathy for the other woman twisted in her chest. "Would you care to join us?"

Reva's expression shifted, and for a brief moment, Faith saw longing in her gray eyes. She understood what it was like to be on the outside looking in, wanting to belong.

How many times had she herself looked at Vinnie's family and wanted to belong? They'd never let her in. And in retrospect, she was again thankful. Had she been attached to his family, would she have had the courage to flee when she needed to?

"Oh, Luke has shown me those before," Reva said airily, her chin going up slightly as if challenging them to dispute her.

"That was nice of him," Faith offered with compassion aching in her heart.

Reva smiled tightly and moved away from the door but instead of going back into the kitchen, she disappeared down the dark hall.

"I'm surprised she came back." Dottie sighed. "I wish she'd get her own life."

Now that Faith knew Reva's situation and had

heard Luke tell her the exact same thing, the wariness Faith had felt for Reva evaporated. "She seems lonely."

The shrill sound of the phone echoed through the house.

"Would you mind getting that, dear?" Dottie leaned back in her chair.

"Sure." Faith stood.

Just then Reva came sailing back into the room. "I'll get the phone," she threw over her shoulder before disappearing into the kitchen.

A moment later she reappeared. "It's for you."

Dottie began to rise, but Reva shook her head. "Not you, Dottie. The phone's for Faith. You can take it in the kitchen." Reva left the room and went back down the dark hall.

Faith couldn't seem to make her feet move. She could feel the blood rushing from her head. Who could be calling?

"Do you want me to find out who it is?" Concern etched lines in Dottie's forehead.

"No, that's okay." The last thing she wanted was for Dottie to think something was wrong. She forced herself to walk, dread creeping into her soul with each step. "It's probably just the pharmacist. I refilled your meds yesterday." Though why they'd be calling now, she didn't know. The pharmacist had assured her the refill would be ready for pick up tomorrow.

In the kitchen the phone lay on the counter, Faith stared at the instrument with apprehension before picking up the receiver and putting it to her ear. "Hello?"

There was a moment of silence before a deep, muffled voice she couldn't identify spoke. "I'm coming for you, Faith. You can't get away from me. No matter where you go, I'll find you."

The line went dead.

Icy talons of fear pierced Faith's skin, causing goose bumps to rise. She dropped the receiver. It clattered noisily on the counter and she backed away. Blood and fear pounded in her brain, her vision blurred.

Tears welled in her eyes and she bit her lip. A trickle of blood seeped into her mouth, the coppery taste making her gag. She hadn't tasted her own blood since the night she'd run away. Violent shudders racked her body and her breathing became shallow.

She had to leave.

But how? Where would she go? Part of her wanted to give up. When would it ever end? Would she ever find the peace she so desperately sought?

The thought of leaving the Campbells' weakened her knees, but for their sake, their safety, she had to go. Her sanctuary was nothing more than a house of cards. God wasn't watching over her. She had to take care of herself and protect those around her. Never mind her selfish dreams.

"Faith, honey, are you all right?" Dottie called from the living room.

It took several tries before she managed to answer, "I'll be right there."

Her mind frantically reviewed her options. She could walk to town and catch a bus. But she'd have to ask Luke or Dottie for some cash. Or she could take some money from her trust fund. Since Vinnie already knew where she was, that seemed the best option.

Only she wouldn't be able to get at the money unless she went to the bank. She'd have to go to town with Luke tomorrow.

Calming herself down enough to rejoin Dottie, Faith settled back on the couch, aware of Dottie's scrutiny.

"You look a little pale," Dottie commented. "Is something wrong?"

"I think I need some fresh air. Would you like to go outside?" Faith asked, hoping to distract Dottie.

Dottie slowly stood. "I'd love to see my babies."

They bundled up and then stepped outside. The snow from the previous evening had dusted the gravel drive, making the uneven surface look more like a sea of scattered marshmallows rather than chunks of stones.

They approached the fence and the llamas meandered over. Brandy came bounding out of the barn to give Faith and Dottie wet kisses before running back to the barn and disappearing inside.

"Luke must still be in with Lucy," Dottie commented.

Faith ran her hands through the soft fur of the animal named Ricky and wished the soothing texture could smooth the edges of her nerves.

"He likes you," Dottie stated. "Ricky is usually very standoffish."

"The llamas are much friendlier than I heard they were," Faith said.

"Faith, Faith!"

Reva's high-pitched call sent the llamas scattering. Reva came hurrying out from the house and down the road, her frosted curls bouncing about in disarray. She'd donned her black, fur-lined parka.

Reva gave Dottie a tight smile. "You're looking the picture of health."

"I feel good." Dottie smiled back brightly and Faith was sure Reva's eyes narrowed slightly before she turned to address her.

"I almost forgot. This was delivered for you on Friday." Reva held out a white envelope.

Faith took it and frowned. "Who delivered it?"

"Oh, some local rug rat. Said some man in town paid him to ride his dirt bike out here."

"When?" Faith looked toward the road. A boy had biked to the ranch and she hadn't seen or heard him? A small tremor raced from Faith's toes to her hand and her throat tightened. She was getting too complacent, too comfortable.

"I don't remember. I'm not your secretary," Reva groused.

Faith inclined her head to acknowledge that. "Well, uh—thanks."

"Aren't you going to open it?" A thread of impatience vibrated in Reva's tone.

Faith didn't want to. A sense of foreboding invaded her senses. First the phone call, now this?

Sliding her fingernail beneath the seal, she slowly opened the envelope and pulled out the folded piece of paper. Her hand shook as she unfolded the note. The words, written in bold, black ink, were in stark contrast to the white paper.

You can't hide from me.

Dizziness clouded Faith's vision, forcing her to lean against the fence for support.

"What is it?" Concern laced Dottie's voice.

"Yes, what is it?" Reva echoed.

Faith's mind worked to come up with a plausible explanation. "It's—just—hmm—personal."

She hated dodging Dottie, but she couldn't tell her the truth. The note was meant to scare her and it was doing a good job. But the note and the phone call wasn't Vinnie's style. He wouldn't give her a chance to run, he'd show up unexpectedly.

It had to be from the private investigator.

Maybe he thought he could flush her out with the note. She glanced down the road. There were no cars visible, but that didn't mean he couldn't be out there somewhere, waiting. She couldn't wait for tomorrow. She had to leave tonight.

Anxious to get back inside and plan her next move, Faith turned to Dottie. "Would you mind if we go back in? I'm feeling a little tired."

"Of course not, dear." Dottie hovered over Faith as if she were the invalid. "We'll get you to your room so you can lie down."

"Oh, yes. You do look a little under the weather." Reva smiled sweetly before walking away.

"That woman has no heart," Dottie muttered, taking Faith's arm.

Faith shrugged and let Dottie lead her back to the

house. After hanging up their coats, Faith asked, "Do you wish to go upstairs?"

"Yes, I think I'll take a rest, as well," Dottie answered.

Faith settled Dottie in her room and turned to leave.

"Whatever it is, Faith, tell Luke."

Stunned, Faith gaped. "I—don't—what?"

With an amazingly strong grip, Dottie took her hand. "Honey, something's got you scared. First, that phone call this afternoon, and now this note. You're pale, and you're shaking like a leaf in the breeze. You don't have to tell me, but tell Luke. He can help you."

Faith closed her eyes. Everything inside screamed for her to do as Dottie suggested, but she couldn't. It wasn't his problem to solve. She kissed Dottie's cheek. "Goodbye."

"Excuse me?" Dottie's anxious expression tore at Faith's heart.

"I mean I'll see you later."

She went to her room to plan. She'd have to make do with the little money she had until she could get to a bank.

Now, if she could just get out without anyone questioning her. Her mind kicked into overdrive. Reva would be leaving the ranch to return to her own home soon.

Fleetingly, Faith contemplated asking Reva for a ride, but discarded the idea. It would be better if no one knew how or why she left. That way when Vinnie did show up, they could honestly say they didn't know what had happened to her. She couldn't leave until dark and when no one would miss her right away.

Once Dottie was upstairs and settled for the night, she'd leave. Luke would be with the llamas or the horses as he always was after dinner, so she'd have to be careful going down the drive.

She'd be leaving the Circle C Ranch tonight and leaving behind a part of her heart.

NINE

From the corner of his eye, Luke saw movement.

He sank back into the shadows and waited. The light of the moon reflecting off the snow illuminated a figure scurrying behind his Bronco. A second later, the person emerged from around the front.

Adrenaline pumped through his heart, energizing him. On quiet feet, he moved through the shadows, closing the gap between him and the mystery person. Approaching from behind, Luke judged the person to be of medium height and slight of frame.

He couldn't make out the face, obscured from his view by a dark cap pulled low over the collar of a dark jacket. The person's pace accelerated, soft tennis shoes crunched slightly on the packed snow on the edge of the gravel drive.

With grim determination, he closed in on his target. No one tried to make off with something from the Campbell ranch. Then he recognized the suitcases.

Confused, he frowned and grabbed Faith by the

scruff of the neck and turned her around. "What are you doing?" he demanded.

Faith dropped the bags and squeaked, "Luke."

"For crying out loud, Faith." Apprehension tightened his chest, making his voice gruff. "Where are you going?"

Her chin came up in a defensive gesture that set his teeth on edge. "I don't have to answer to you."

"Oh, yes you do." He grabbed the bags. "We'll discuss this inside."

"Give me my luggage." Faith struggled unsuccessfully to take the bags from his grip. Finally, she fisted her hand. "You have no right to stop me, Luke Campbell."

Anger and an odd sense of hurt flashed within his chest. Had the friendship they'd begun to build mean nothing? "Oh no? I think I have every right. As your employer, I deserve two weeks' notice." He thought she might be on the verge of tears, but he couldn't tell for sure.

"I don't have two weeks!"

Her exclamation left him more bewildered and he softened his tone. "As your friend, I'd like to know what's going on."

She turned away from him and the moon's glow lit her features, exposing her drawn, scared expression. That did it. He would get answers out of her tonight, even if he needed to throw her over his shoulder and carry her inside.

"Come on, Faith. We're going in."

He could tell by the tightening of her lips that she wanted to protest. Giving her no chance, he turned on his heel and carried her bags toward the house. He let out an exaggerated sigh when she didn't immediately follow, but when he heard her quiet footfalls behind him, he released a quick breath of relief.

Bossy, controlling, arrogant.

Faith couldn't come up with enough names to silently yell at Luke's retreating back.

Didn't he realize she had to go for his sake? *No, of course not, you dolt.* He didn't know what lurked out there, waiting to pounce. She hadn't told him.

She stoically followed him into the study. The overhead light came on bathing the room in a yellow ambient glow. He went around the wide walnut desk and set her bags down on the muted sage green carpet before seating himself in his black leather captain's chair.

"Please, shut the door."

His tone made her think of the one time she'd been sent to the dean's office in prep school for talking in class. Luke had that same reasonable look on his face that Dean Snoddgrass had had, and it made her feel small and insecure. But she was a grown woman, not a child.

And she'd vowed after Vinnie, she would never cower before a man again.

Drawing herself to her full height of five-feet, eight-inches tall, she closed the door and moved to sit on the striped cushioned divan by the window. Looking at Luke, she clasped her hands in front of her and waited.

"You do that when you're nervous." Luke leaned forward, his look intent.

"Do what?"

"Clasp your hands together until the knuckles turn white." He nodded toward her hands.

Abashed, she looked down and realized her knuckles were indeed turning white. Unhooking her fingers, she spread her hands, palms down, on her thighs.

"So tell me," he said.

Biting her lip, she hedged. "Tell you what?"

For a long, silent moment he closed his eyes, and when he opened them she knew he'd reached the end of his patience. "Tell me what's really going on."

"I don't have to tell you anything." Surprised at herself for baiting him, she steeled herself for his reaction. Her heart told her Luke was a man who had control of his temper, yet when his palms landed on the desk, making a loud noise, she flinched.

"I can't help you, Faith, unless you tell me what you're so afraid of. And don't tell me it's investors or charitable organizations," he said through gritted teeth.

"Who said I wanted your help?" Though that was exactly what she wanted.

She wanted to break down and let him take care of everything. It was so hard to be strong and brave. And alone. But she cared too much about him to continue to risk his safety.

He came around the desk, moving slowly and deliberately. She tensed, steeling herself as old fears rushed headlong into her mind. Was she wrong about him? Would he be like Vinnie and use his physical power to bend her to his will?

Luke knelt down beside her and took her hands in his. Relief swept through her and burning tears gathered at the back of her eyes. He'd proven himself gentle and self-controlled before. She was ashamed for doubting him.

"Whatever your burdens are, God can help you. Tell him. And if I can help you, I will."

Each word he spoke was a plea to her heart. She could feel the tears gathering steam and fought them with all her might. God wouldn't help her. What right did she have to put Luke in danger? What right did she have to his help? She tried to speak. "I—I don't—"

"Please, Faith."

The tenderness of his voice battered down her defenses and she broke, like a water pipe bursting. Large, wet tears streamed down her face and sobs racked her body. The brave front, the unyielding control she'd kept herself under, shattered like crystal hitting the floor. Jagged edges of pain and fear cut into her, leaving her wounded and bleeding inside.

The past had caught up with her, the uncertainty of the future stretched out before her and the world seemed more cold, more desolate than before.

Luke gathered her into his arms and suddenly warmth enveloped her, a soothing balm to her tattered soul. The embrace was comforting and the pressure secure. His hand stroked down her back in a calming tempo. The rhythmic movement continued until the tide of tears ebbed and the flow dried up. She lifted her head from his shoulder and their gazes locked.

The air around them seemed to shift and change, the embrace became a caress and heat scorched her palms where they rested against his hard chest. Faith took a shuddering breath, unsure what she should do.

Luke's smile was as intimate as a kiss and the effect left her off-kilter.

Gathering her strength, she sniffed. "I don't usually cry on men's shoulders."

"No, I don't suppose you do. I would imagine you don't let anyone close enough." He tucked a lock of hair behind her ear, the gesture raising goose bumps on her skin.

"I'm sorry." How she hated that sentiment. She'd sworn to herself she wouldn't say those words anymore. For too many years those little words spared her some pain, but not humiliation.

Luke shook his head. "You have nothing to be sorry for."

Everything was turned upside down. Her strength deserted her. "You don't understand."

"Make me understand." His words caressed her.

"Where do I begin?" she whispered, her voice raw.

"Start with tonight. Why were you leaving?"

A sense of the inevitable overwhelmed her and her head dropped to his chest. Luke's finger under her chin brought her gaze back to his. From deep inside she dredged up the courage to tell him. "He's coming."

"Who?"

Taking a deep breath, she blurted out the truth. "My ex-husband."

Instantly, an oppressive weight lifted from her, making her light-headed. And just as quickly, she felt guilty for her utter selfishness. Her motivation for telling him wasn't to protect him and his family but to lighten her own load.

She expected him to recoil, to draw away from her, but he touched her cheek with the back of his finger, his voice soft. "He's who you're running from?"

She nodded.

"How do you know he's coming here?"

"He called."

It sounded ridiculous and it still didn't seem right. It just wasn't Vinnie's style to give any warning. He usually struck when least expected.

"Are you sure the voice was his?"

Faith frowned. "I—the voice was muffled, but who else could it have been?"

Luke stood and began to pace. "What did he say?"

"Well—" She bit her lip in concentration. "If I remember correctly, he said, 'I'm coming for you, Faith. You can't get away. No matter where you go, I'll find you.'"

"Could the call have been from someone else?" Luke sounded unconvinced.

"I don't know." Faith realized her hands were clasped tight again. Quickly, she separated them.

"The P.I., maybe?"

She shrugged. "I had the same thought, but why would he do that?"

Then she remembered the note. She pulled it out

of her pocket and offered the folded piece of paper to Luke. "This was also delivered here."

He took the note and read it in silence. His jaw tightened and the small scar on his chin blanched.

"You said this was delivered?" He looked up from the note and studied her.

She nodded.

"By who?"

"A boy."

"When?"

"Sometime Friday."

"What did he say?" The questions came like rapid fire.

"That some man paid him to ride his bike out and deliver the note."

"You talked to the boy?"

He should have been a lawyer, she thought. "No, Reva did."

His eyes narrowed. "I'll talk with her tomorrow." Stroking his chin, he seemed deep in thought.

This is it, she thought, he's going to tell me to leave. What choice did he have? He had to do it to protect Dottie, himself and all the rest of them. Faith closed her eyes, confused why the knowledge hurt so much. She'd been on her way when he'd stopped her, so what did it matter?

It mattered because before it had been her decision, now it would be his.

"Why is your ex-husband looking for you? The money you were talking about?"

Opening her eyes, she met his intense stare. How

did she explain the crazed mind of Vince Palmero? "No, not the money. He wants what belongs to him."

Luke moved to his desk and leaned his hips against the edge. "Meaning?"

Faith stood and did some pacing of her own. She retraced her steps several times before she finally found it within herself to go on. "Meaning, he is a possessive man who never lets anything be taken away from him."

Unable to face Luke, she continued her trek back and forth across the room. "You have to understand that I was his ticket to a life he'd only been able to view from the outside. Through me, he was able to enter New York society. When I left him it was the ultimate betrayal. To him, I am a possession. Nothing more than a showpiece, bought and paid for through marriage. The money is just a bonus."

The ache in her tightly clenched hands barely registered against the ache inside. She faced Luke, not sure what to expect. His dark eyes were hooded and hiding any indication of his thoughts. Doggedly, she continued. "I am his property, Luke, and he won't rest until I'm back in my gilded cage." She shuddered. "Or dead."

"Neither one of those things is going to happen, Faith."

He sounded so sure, she longed to believe him. "He's not going to stop looking for me. I should leave now while I can before he comes here. He's unpredictable. I'm sorry I put you and your family in danger."

Ignoring her words, he asked, "What have the police done?"

She lifted her hands in the air in a helpless gesture. "The police? Are you kidding? In New York, you have to prove abuse for a divorce to be granted on the grounds of cruel and inhumane treatment. So my lawyer filed for separation, and then a year later I was granted a divorce based on that. But in the meantime, Vinnie began stalking me."

She gave a mirthless laugh. "Or I should say he had others stalk me. Again, for an order of protection to be granted, I had to prove *he* was stalking me. One officer I talked to had been sympathetic and suggested a bodyguard."

She clenched her fists. Ineffectual rage at the system burned hot in her soul. "Brian, the bodyguard, ended up in the hospital with a bullet in his back. Of course, there were no witnesses and the police said they had no evidence implicating Vinnie. It was then I realized the only way to protect myself and everyone near me was to run. Unfortunately, that was the one night Vinnie decided to make his move. He must have had someone watching me because he showed up just as I was leaving."

She hated even thinking about that night. "He— he hurt me badly. But I still got away. And once again since there were no witnesses, just my word against his and he had an alibi—his family—the police's hands were tied."

Nothing she said seemed to faze Luke. He still leaned motionless against the desk, his expression indecipherable.

She repeated her earlier words. "I should leave."

Suddenly he pushed away from the desk, tension emanating from him in waves. He shook his head. "Running isn't the answer. Just because there are no walls, you're still in a cage."

"But Luke, you don't seem to understand. He's coming *here*. I've put you and your family in danger. I have to go."

A sinking feeling told her he wanted to play the hero and an image of Brian, on the ground, blood seeping from the wound in his back, skittered across her mind. "I couldn't stand it if I were responsible for some harm done to you or your mother."

"Nothing is going to happen to any of us, Faith." He stood in front of the window and stared out at the black night.

"Do you honestly believe you can protect us from Vinnie?" She continued on even though he kept his back to her and didn't respond. "You would tower over him, but what good is that when faced with a gun?"

Still no response. She frowned and said, "My only option is to keep running." She moved around the desk to pick up her bags.

In the reflection of the window, she noticed Luke had closed his eyes and his lips moved with silent words. She stilled. He was praying. She was awed by the thought that he was asking God for help. "No use praying on my account. God wants nothing to do with me."

He turned then. "That's not true, Faith. God loves

you very much. And we will figure this out. I need to know everything you can tell me about Vinnie."

"Luke, this isn't your problem. This isn't a military operation for you to understand and execute. This is my life."

"And I need to get a handle on the situation so we can determine the best course of action."

"I'm not asking you to help me, Luke. I'm asking you to let me go. Just forget you ever met me."

He shook his head. "I can't do that. God brought you into my life for a reason."

"It was chance that brought me into your life, not God."

"Do you really believe that?"

"I don't know what to believe anymore." Since she'd landed in Oregon and met Luke, she'd felt closer to God, thought she'd felt His presence through Luke and Dottie. But why now after all these years?

He considered her words. "Tell me what happened with your marriage."

To humor him, she complied. She avoided his gaze as shame washed over her. "Vinnie wasn't what I thought he was when I married him."

"What did you think he was?"

"I thought he was a good man." She shrugged. "When my grandfather died, I was so lost and alone. I fell apart. Vinnie worked for the law firm that handled Grandfather's estate. He was so—smooth. At first, kind and sympathetic. He stayed by my side during the funeral and the following days when so many people came around demanding money. I mistook my gratitude for love. When he asked me to marry him it seemed like the right thing to do. By the time I realized how wrong I'd been about him, it was too late. He'd wanted what marrying me could bring him."

She glanced at Luke. He sat attentively listening. No one had ever really listened to her before.

"He'd known just how to play me. I was so gullible."

"Go on," Luke prodded gently.

"He never quite fit in to the New York social circles. Oh, he got invited to the best parties and had access to the most exclusive clubs, but he couldn't change the fact that he'd grown up in a blue-collar home in the Bronx. And he became obsessed with me. He wanted to control my every move, who I talked to, where I went. I found myself becoming more and more isolated from the world until I felt like a prisoner in my own home."

"So you broke free."

She gave a mirthless laugh. "No, not right away, but I should have. Instead I thought I could change him, make him see how unhealthy his behavior was getting. But the more I tried, the worse he got." A shudder rippled down her spine. "One day I tried too hard."

"What did he do?" Luke's voice sounded gruff and his expression fierce.

Her throat constricted making her unable to continue. She shook her head, wanting to run, to get away from the memories.

"Did he hit you, Faith?"

"He—he hurt—me." She remembered the look of

rage on Vinnie's face, the sound of his fists slamming into her body, and the pain. The pain that still lingered in her shoulder and her heart.

"Did you tell the police this?"

"Vinnie kept me under lock and key most of the time. I couldn't go to the police. Besides, he was smart enough not to hit where it would be obvious. At first I tried to understand and believed his promises that it wouldn't happen again." She clenched her fists. "I'd turned into one of those women you see in made-for-TV movies. He may have hurt me in so many ways, but he never crushed me."

She could see the anger in his eyes and the tightening of his jaw. "Faith, you were right to leave him. God would not expect you to stay in an abusive relationship."

Fresh tears gathered in her eyes. She'd been taught that marriage was for life. No matter what.

His expression softened. He took her hands again. "God loves you, Faith. God did not author the evil that has touched your life. The Bible urges believers to separate from those who hurt them and to create a safe place for themselves. And you've done that, Faith."

"If God loves me, why did He allow it?" Old anger surfaced, clogging her throat. She didn't understand. She'd tried to be good. A good daughter, a good granddaughter, a good wife. Still He'd taken her parents and then her grandparents away. He hadn't protected her from Vinnie.

Luke squeezed her hands and looked at her with an earnestness that touched her soul. "I don't have the answer to that question, Faith. He never promised there wouldn't be difficult, awful times in our lives, but He promised to be there with us. He knows you and He has cried with you. He has felt your hurt and your anguish. He's not sitting up in the sky judging you, looking for ways to hurt you. He loves you. He wants you to put your trust in Him."

The crystal blue of Luke's eyes shimmered. Faith swallowed as the tears gathered in her own eyes. She wanted to believe Luke's words, she just felt so uncertain and lost.

"Faith, it wasn't chance or coincidence that brought you here. I know in my heart that God has a plan for you. You just need to lay down your doubts and trust."

"That's easier said than done."

Luke smiled tenderly. "It takes a leap of faith."

"I suppose it does."

She held his gaze and the moment stretched. In the depths of Luke's eyes, she could see and feel the mercy and grace of God's love. She felt warmed and cared for and she would take the memories of this moment with her, because, sadly, the situation had not changed. "Luke, I appreciate your words, I really do. But it doesn't change the fact that I need to leave. And I need to leave now."

He shook his head. She could feel the tension inside of him. He stood and paced. When he stopped he looked at her with a determined light in his eyes. "We don't have to decide anything tonight. Tomorrow, after we've had a chance to think things through, then we can—" He paused and stepped closer. "We, together, will figure out a way to protect you. You can't keep running for the rest of your life."

She stood. "I don't think—"

"Please, promise me you'll rest tonight and tomorrow we can deal with all of this."

Leaving in the morning would be easier. Luke could take her to town; she could stop at the bank and then catch the next bus. "All right."

Luke looked relieved. He moved to his desk and pulled something from one of the drawers. When he came back to her, he held a leather-bound Bible in his hands. "My father gave this to me when I was a teenager. I'd like you to have it."

"Oh, Luke, I couldn't." Her grandfather had had a beautiful Bible that he'd read from and in those last few weeks she'd taken to reading the psalms to him.

"Please." He put the book in her hands.

Awed by the gift, Faith ran her finger over the inscription in the bottom right hand corner. TO MY SON, LUKE CAMPBELL.

"I think you'll find the answers you seek in there."

Faith's gaze shot to Luke's. How did he know? "I wouldn't know where to begin."

"I've always been partial to the book of Luke myself." He grinned.

She laughed. "That sounds like a good place to start."

Luke's expression turned serious. "In the morning, we'll come up with a plan."

"I need to stay longer."

"Oh, nice joke. When are you coming back?"

"It's no joke, Rog." Luke could picture his friend's chocolate-brown forehead creased with lines and his black eyes narrowing as silence stretched over the phone line. Though Roger Tumble was his commanding officer, their friendship had been immediate and tight. Each attributed the deep bond to their mutual commitment to God.

In his soft southern drawl, Roger commented, "How much time?"

"End of January."

"I'll send you the paperwork. Your mom not doing well?"

"She's good. Something else has come up."

"Now, that sounds intriguing. Care to share?"

Luke stared out the window of his office and watched snow fall against the dark sky. Light-colored flecks floated down to earth, blanketing the ground. Good thing he'd stopped Faith from leaving or she'd be trudging through the snow right now. "Not really."

"Don't tell me this has anything to do with a woman?"

Luke sighed. "It does."

"I could have sworn you were a confirmed bachelor. So tell me."

Luke grimaced. He wasn't ready to discuss the issue of Faith yet. Not when his emotions were all over the place. "When I see you."

There was a pause. "If that's what you want. Give your mother my best."

"I will. How's the weekly Bible study going?"

"So, so. It's not the same without your leadership."

Luke felt a blast of guilt for leaving the guys in the field for so long.

He'd worked so hard to build a foundation of ministry in his unit; he didn't want it to flounder.

But right now Faith needed him more.

"Thanks, Roger. I'll talk with you soon." He hung up and sat back.

For most of the night, he'd wrestled with his conflicting thoughts about Faith, about the secrets she'd kept and about the potential danger she'd brought to his house. He was angry. Sure. Her presence put his mother in harm's way. Though, the threat was slim compared to the war he'd been fighting on the other side of the world.

But more, he was hurt that Faith hadn't confided in him sooner.

Earlier he'd contacted the sheriff and filled him in. Sheriff Bane had checked out the P.I. The Sheriff had assured Luke that Costello had left town. Sheriff Bane said he'd keep an eye out for any other strangers. Also, he'd promised to send a car along the main road at intervals.

After talking to the sheriff, Luke had contacted a local lawyer who said he'd see what he could do legally to protect Faith.

Now all he had to do was convince Faith to stay put and to keep his own heart from falling victim to her.

TEN

Rats! Large rats with heavy feet in the attic. Faith's pulse raced. Panic rushed in.

Something. Someone was on the roof. Trying to get in. Vinnie?

She scrambled out of bed. She was shaking so hard, she had trouble pulling on her robe and putting her feet into her tennis shoes. At the bedroom door, she paused and listened. The quietness of the hall suggested all was well. But she knew what she'd heard. She hurried to Luke's door and knocked. No answer.

Biting her lip to keep the panic from overwhelming her, she cautiously went downstairs. Faint streaks of the dawn light splintered through the cracks in the curtains. The frigid air left from the night clawed at her, prickling her skin.

With her hand on the knob leading outside, she paused. The noise she'd heard earlier became recognizable. She stepped outside and followed the steady beat of a hammer around the house until she was standing just below her bedroom window.

On the ground was a pile of clean snow, obviously cleared from the roof. She arched her back and craned her neck to see onto the roof. A male was crouched with a hammer in his hand.

Her shoulders sagged with relief. "Luke, what are you doing?"

The hammering stopped and he stood. "Blocking the vents so the raccoons don't nest," he replied.

The dawn light bathed Luke in its frosty glow. He had a cap pulled low over his ears. His usually clean-shaven face showed the night's growth of beard, making him more rugged and handsome. Traces of snow clung to his work boots and his thick plaid shirt didn't look nearly warm enough.

"It's barely five o'clock in the morning. I nearly had a heart attack!"

"Sorry," he called. "I couldn't sleep."

"It's freezing, not to mention that roof is slick with ice. You're going to kill yourself up there. Come down."

He regarded her for a moment. "Worried, are you?"

Heat crawled up her neck. "As I would be of anyone standing on an icy roof."

With a grin, he stated, "I'll be done soon. Then we can talk."

"Fine," she replied and pulled her robe tighter against the chilly air.

She'd let him talk her into staying last night, but she was determined to leave today. No matter how much she didn't want to.

* * *

The sharp winter sun beat down on Luke. Even though the temperature barely reached thirty degrees, beads of sweat rolled down his back and disappeared into the waistband of his jeans.

He'd long since removed his flannel shirt, opting for just a long-sleeved thermal. And now he used the edge of the material to wipe his brow as he stood to stretch his tired muscles. His gaze took in the beauty of the land.

The looming Cascade mountain range covered in lush forests of Ponderosa Pines dusted white was breathtaking. The high desert, though flat, stretched out with a beauty of its own, whether in winter or during the blush of spring or the heat of a dry summer or the turning of the leaves in fall. It didn't matter the time of year, he loved this land.

Luke knelt down and picked up a tile, turning it over in his hands the same way his conflicted thoughts turned in his head.

He should be back with his unit, fighting the good fight to keep freedom a reality for all human life. Helping the men to keep their faith.

Yet, he wanted to stay here where his life began.

He wanted to fulfill the dream his father had for him. But which father?

His earthly father had wanted him to run this ranch, to carry on the Campbell name and pass on the legacy of love that his parents had built. Blake Campbell had never made his wishes for his son a secret.

His Heavenly Father had wanted Luke to join

the military, to serve his country as well as serve God. Luke had never made his faith a secret and he'd gladly done as he felt the Lord wanted of him, never once feeling unsure of his path.

But now Luke *was* unsure. Why had the Lord brought Faith into his life? And why was he so glad?

The tile fell from his hands like a hot coal. Was he falling for Faith? The emotions bouncing around his head and his heart were unfamiliar. And, frankly, it scared him. *Lord, what's happening? Is this part of Your plan? But why?*

He liked Faith and respected her. He admired her courage and strength, was proud of how capable and willing she was to try new things. Her sense of humor and quick wit captivated him. And yes, he was physically attracted to her. Any male with a beating heart and blood in his veins would be. Kissing her had only solidified that attraction.

But falling for her? No way.

Picking up his hammer, he pounded the nails in the last vent with more force than necessary. He had to get perspective here.

It would only complicate matters if he were to pursue any type of relationship with Faith beyond that of friend. She had baggage in her past that needed to be dealt with, and he had a life to sort out. It wouldn't work for them to get involved.

He was a man used to being in control. He could control himself, all of him, including his emotions.

Awareness brushed over him as Faith walked outside again. As if the world had suddenly slowed on its axis, he stood to watch her walk to the fence. Three llamas trotted instantly to her side.

Sunlight danced off her girlish ponytail, making her look young and carefree. His throat constricted, trapping his breath in his chest, painfully expanding his lungs. It pleased him to see she wore the down parka he'd picked up for her in town. Much better suited to the climate than the thin wool coat she'd arrived in.

Suddenly the fence railing inches from Faith exploded with a dull thud, splintering the wood into flying junks. The llamas scattered. Faith yelped and crouched low, covering her head with her hands. Close to her feet, dirt and snow sprayed out as something hit the ground.

Gunfire!

Panic seized Luke's lungs. His gaze frantically searched for the shooter as he stepped forward. On the main road a dark green pickup screeched away.

Luke's foot slipped on the slick roof and he realized he'd made a mistake. He went down hard on his backside, then onto his back. His hands flayed hopelessly in search of something to grab, his body plummeted down the roof, the edges of each tile biting into his flesh. His teeth ground together in sharp pain.

From below him, he heard Faith's cry of alarm.

The gutter rushed at him and he grabbed hold, but one end of the metal gave way with a loud wrenching creak. His grip failed and he was free-falling again.

Then he hit the snow-covered ground with a dull

thud and a loud groan. The last thing he saw before his eyes slid shut was the hunk of gutter swaying over his head.

He was dead.

Fear constricted Faith's heart, forced the air from her lungs. She ran to him, to his limp body on the snow-covered ground.

"Oh, please don't let him be dead."

Putting her fingers against his neck, she felt a strong pulse beating a steady rhythm and momentary relief eased her panic.

He wasn't dead.

"Luke? Luke, can you hear me?"

She quickly searched his body for broken bones. There didn't seem to be any obvious fractures. But his head…she stifled a sob.

"Luke—" Her voice trailed off and tears sprang to her eyes. "God, let him be all right, please."

With jerky, harsh movements, she wiped away her tears. *He's not going to die,* she admonished herself gruffly. God would not do that to Luke.

He needed help and she was his only hope. She stood and turned to run, but a hand wrapped around her ankle nearly toppled her over. She screamed before noticing Luke regarding her with pain-filled eyes. Immediately she knelt beside him.

"I have to go—get h-help." Her voice broke.

"I'm—okay," he croaked on a deep breath before wincing.

Faith smoothed a hand over his brow. "You're hurt."

"Minor scrapes and bruises."

"You might have a broken back or neck, even."

"The snow broke my fall," he quipped. "Are you okay?"

A ripple of terror ran through her. "Yes. Thankfully he was a bad shot."

"Not meant to kill, only scare."

"Well, then, he did a good job. Let me go get help." She moved to rise again, but his hand gripped her arm.

"You help me."

"Luke, you shouldn't move, not until the ambulance comes."

He closed his eyes. "I've fallen off that roof more times than I can count. It just knocked the wind out of me."

"I don't know." She looked him over, unconvinced. "I still think I should get a doctor."

With a groan, Luke pushed himself up on to his elbows. His eyes scrunched up tight and his mouth thinned. The scar on his jaw paled. His visible pain made her nauseous.

With infinite care, he sat. The rip in his shirt revealed a raw cut on his shoulder. So much red. The sight of his blood turned her stomach. It could have been so much worse. For both of them.

And that's when it hit her.

If anything happened to Luke she knew her heart wouldn't survive.

She helped him stand and when his arm settled around her shoulders, she staggered slightly as she bore the brunt of his weight.

They entered the house and Faith steered him to a chair at the kitchen table. "Do you have a first-aid kit somewhere? We need to clean your wounds."

Grimacing, he lowered himself to the chair. "I need the phone."

She handed the phone over and clenched her hands together as he called the sheriff to explain what had happened.

When he hung up, she asked, "Do you think they'll catch him?"

"We can pray so." He started to rise. "I have a first-aid kit in my room."

She rushed to support him as they made their way upstairs. "Should I get your mother? She was sleeping when I came outside."

"If she didn't hear anything, let's not upset her."

Pushing open the door of his bedroom, she realized she'd never before seen his domain. His masculine scent swirled around her, heightening her already taut senses.

He pointed to the closet. "My first-aid kit's in there."

The kit sat on the floor of the closet next to his cowboy boots. She also grabbed a soft-looking blue flannel shirt off the hanger. On the verge of closing the door, her gaze snagged on a blur of green.

It hit her like a punch in the stomach.

These were his military clothes—camouflage fatigues with his name sewn on the breast pocket and a dark green suit. Even in the dim light of the bedroom, the medals and ribbons were eye-catching.

At the reminder of his life outside the ranch an

ache in the vicinity of her heart stole her breath away. Resolutely, she turned away, telling herself she shouldn't be upset. She'd known from the beginning that Luke was only a temporary fixture in her life. One day soon he'd be leaving, going back to a job where worse than a fall from a roof could happen. Where his life would be in danger every second.

Masking her distress, she moved back to the bed and set the kit down. The case easily opened with a click and she pulled out the supplies she needed. Unable to meet Luke's gaze, she handed him two painkillers. "I'll go get you some water."

Luke shook his head. "Not necessary." He popped the pills into his mouth and swallowed them dry.

The large cut on his shoulder needed her attention first. She helped him to remove his shirt and forced her gaze to stay on the cut, not on the width of his shoulders and muscles on his arms. Thankful for something to keep her mind and hands busy, she doused a cotton pad with an antiseptic. Before applying the pad to his skin, she said, "This may sting."

He nodded and she placed the soaked pad against his flesh.

Luke closed his eyes but made no noise.

Taking her lip between her teeth, Faith continued to bathe the wound, wondering at his ability to take the pain. Once the area was free from the dried blood, she used butterfly bandages to close the gap.

Tenderly, she began to tend to the various other bloodied scrapes. A nasty looking scar on his right shoulder caught her attention. The skin puckered and drew inward around what appeared to have been some sort of hole. Faith went rigid.

An image of her bodyguard flashed in her mind. With shaky hands, she touched the imperfect flesh. Hoping it wasn't what she feared, she asked, "What is this?"

Luke shrugged. "Got too close to a pitchfork one day."

"A pitchfork," she repeated, her voice breaking.

His head swiveled around and he stared at her for a long tense moment. Faith looked back at him steadily, knowing his flippant remark was meant to deflect, but she was unwilling to push for the truth.

Still holding her gaze, he stated flatly, "It's a bullet wound."

Having the truth confirmed did nothing to ease the distress she felt. She placed her hand over the scar as if she could somehow erase the proof of his mortality.

Feeling his gaze on her again, she lifted her eyes and met his intense look. In a voice barely above a whisper, she said, "Tell me about your life in the army."

He cocked his head to the side. "You want to know about the good parts or the not-so-good parts?"

"All the parts."

"War is ugly." A bleakness entered his expression and the look tore at her heart.

"Where were you when 9/11 happened?" she asked.

"At the time I was stationed in Birmingham, Alabama."

"And then?"

"Afghanistan. Operation Enduring Freedom. I agree with why we went, but I still have to live with the memories."

With a gentle touch she caressed his cheek, wishing she could take away his pain. "How *do* you live with the memories?"

"I release them to Jesus."

She marveled at his trust and dedication to the Lord. She didn't completely understand, but she admired his faith. Maybe one day she'd be as certain of God as Luke was.

"I'm sorry you had to see any fighting at all," she commented softly.

He gave her an odd look.

"What?"

The moment stretched and then finally he spoke as if she'd opened the floodgates to a dam, his words tumbled out, his voice a rough, raw rasp. She could see his torment, could hear the anguish in his tone.

He told her of secret missions long before the tragedy in New York, most in far-off places and some surprisingly closer to home. He talked of lives he'd saved and those he'd taken, and with each story he grew more distant, more mechanical.

Her heart cracked in her chest and she knew any minute it would shatter into a million pieces; her anguish at his private torment was tearing her apart. She touched her fingertip to his lips, stilling his words.

"Why do you stay in the service?" she asked, gently.

"I joined because God led me there. I stay out of obedience to what He has called me to."

The simple honesty in his eyes struck her profoundly. She'd never experienced that kind of certainty in her life.

She helped him into the flannel shirt. Careful not to put pressure on his wounds, she wrapped her arms around him, needing to somehow comfort his soul, as well as his body. For a heartbeat he resisted.

"Let me," she whispered.

He melted against her, coming to rest in the cradle of her arms.

It was a heady feeling, this sense of protectiveness and willingness to give of herself, one she'd never fully experienced before. Oh, she'd cared for her ailing grandfather, but this…this was different. More intense, more…consuming.

She smoothed her hand over his hair. His head rested against her shoulder and the warmth made her feel strong and sure. After a long, silent moment, he lifted his head. The spot where his head had been grew cold, but the look in his eyes warmed her heart.

"Faith, I've never told another person these things before," he wavered. He sounded stunned and a bit frightened.

His openness, his trust was a precious gift. One she didn't deserve, but one she would cherish. "Thank you."

He reached for her and winced.

"You need rest." Purposefully, she made her voice brusque. She'd allow things to get too personal as it was.

Waving away her concern, he said, "Need to see the damage outside from the gunshots."

"We shouldn't go outside," she stated, her heart pounding with fresh panic.

He stood, his jaw tightening. "You shouldn't go outside. Not yet. I need to figure out how to better protect you."

As he moved past her and out the door, tenderness welled inside her chest. She would be forever grateful to God for bringing Luke into her life, for showing her that not all men were the same. Some could be generous, giving, loving. But her feelings for Luke left her no other choice. She had to leave.

No matter how much it would hurt.

Luke stared at the bullet hole. Or rather what remained of the shattered wooden fence railing. Hot coals of anger burned in his gut right alongside ice-cold terror at how close those bullets had come to taking out Faith.

The shooter was no amateur. At the distance that truck had been, he had to have had a high-powered rifle, and the lack of retort suggested a silencer.

The jilted ex-husband?

Luke didn't think so. Not from what Faith had said about him.

A hired assassin? Then why the scare tactic?

Luke's lip curled in disgust. Her husband didn't want her back, he wanted to hunt her down. The man enjoyed the chase.

Luke fisted his hand. He hated the helpless, sitting-duck feeling stealing over him. Action. That's what he needed. Take action. Find Vinnie Palmero and end this situation. Then Faith would be free to go back to her life.

Luke frowned, not liking how the thought of Faith leaving stabbed at him.

Faith needed to leave and resume her life so that *he* could resume his life.

With that in mind, Luke headed to his office and called the sheriff's station again and was told the sheriff was on his way to the Circle C Ranch.

While he waited he did a Google search on Palmero. There was, he found, very little info. His name in the New York Bar Association, a few court cases, a wedding announcement for his marriage to the Delange Heiress.

And one interesting tidbit. An article about a man named Anthony Palmero who had been arrested and put in jail for the robbery and murder of a store clerk. The article mentioned that the younger brother, a lawyer named Vince Palmero, had worked tirelessly to get his brother paroled. He'd been successful. Anthony Palmero was paroled after serving ten of his twenty-year sentence.

Luke wasn't sure how this all fit together with Faith's situation. Funny that she hadn't mentioned Anthony.

Two cars pulled up outside; the sheriff with an entourage.

Luke went out to meet them.

Sheriff Bane and Deputy Unger emerged from the first car. Two other uniformed officers stepped from the second vehicle. Luke knew them, Deputy Jason

Russell and Bill Smith, the county's local crime-scene tech. He acknowledged them with a nod.

"Did you find the truck?" Luke asked as he shook hands with the sheriff.

"Yes. Abandoned on the other side of town. It was stolen sometime during the night from some tourists renting a condo at the Black Butte Resort. The vehicle had been wiped clean."

Luke wasn't surprised. Leo and Jerry came out of the llama barn. Luke filled them in on the morning's events. "Where are Mac and Charles?"

"Mac's visiting his mother over in Bend. I haven't seen Charles today," answered Leo.

"I'll see if he's in his room," Jerry offered.

"I didn't realize Mac was local," Luke stated.

Leo shrugged in answer.

"So that's where the bullets hit?" the sheriff asked as he moved closer to the fence.

"Faith was standing there, where Jason is," Luke commented, pointing.

Deputy Russell whistled. "That was close."

"Okay, Bill. Do your thing," Sheriff Bane said, stepping back to give Bill room to find the slugs. "I'll be posting Jason here outside the gate. He and Deputy Unger will be taking turns. No one will go in or out with out passing them first. I've contacted the New York Department of Justice. They're checking on Palmero. As soon as I learn anything I'll let you know."

"Thanks."

"How's Faith holding up?"

"She's spooked," Luke replied.

"Keep her close to the ranch. If her ex-husband is anywhere in the vicinity, he'll have a hard time getting to her if she's here."

"That won't be a problem." He hoped.

"Good."

"Got them," Bill exclaimed and held up the two small metal bullets between his latex-covered fingers. He bagged the slugs.

"Not much else for us to do now," stated the sheriff. "I'll keep in touch." He, Bill and Deputy Unger climbed into the sheriff's car.

Luke thanked them and watched as they drove out of the drive. Deputy Russell parked his vehicle just outside the Circle C entrance.

"The guys and I will also take turns patrolling the ranch," said Leo, his weathered face showing concern.

Luke nodded his thanks. Grateful for the support.

For now they were safe. But the thrumming of warning pulsing through his veins questioned that reasoning. The threat remained out there, lurking.

And Luke was anxious to meet it head on.

ELEVEN

From the living-room window, Faith watched the uniformed men talk with Luke. The need to confide in Dottie rose sharply. Dottie deserved to know the truth.

Faith took a deep breath. "There's something I have to tell you."

"What it is, dear?" Dottie put down her knitting.

She told Dottie about her ex-husband, about the months of running and finally about Luke's offer of protection.

Dottie listened intently, her gaze never wavering.

Faith wound up her tale and waited for recriminations from Dottie, for the anger and hurt that would come for putting the Campbell family in such danger.

But Dottie surprised her by reaching out and taking her hand. "You poor child. To think you've been alone and scared for so long. I knew when you came here something weighed on your mind. And on your heart."

Faith couldn't comprehend Dottie's compassion. "You aren't mad at me?"

"Of course not. This situation will take care of both of you and Luke's problems."

"Both of our problems?" Faith repeated, confused. What problem did Luke have?

"Yes, Luke needs you as much as you need him." Dottie nodded sagely.

"He does?"

"Of course, dear. He just doesn't know that he does, but I think he's beginning to realize it."

Baffled, Faith felt like she was walking through a maze. Luke needed her? Whatever for?

"My son has been searching for fulfillment for most of his life, Faith. He thought he'd find it in the army. And I'm not saying he didn't find some. I know the military is a great adventure for him, but when he comes home on leave, I see the emptiness. You can't hide some things from a mother." Dottie laughed softly, the corners of her eyes creasing.

"No, I suppose not," Faith agreed, sharing Dottie's smile and turning to watch Luke out the window. The sheriff and his men dispersed, leaving Luke and the hands talking.

Dottie touched her arm. "Since he's been home this time, he's slowly changed. The emptiness isn't so visible. And with you here, he seems—happier."

"Really?" Faith couldn't stop the hope seeping into her heart, the pleasure welling up inside.

Dottie gave her a knowing smile and patted her hand. "He laughs and smiles more readily. In fact, he makes getting you to laugh his mission. And when he doesn't think you're looking, he watches you like a lost soul who has spotted a beacon in the dark."

Faith wanted to believe her, she really did, and in the past few weeks she'd learned how to dream. But in the back of her mind, she knew she was quite possibly setting herself up for more disappointment and heartache.

If only she could focus on the positive.

Wasn't Christmas a time of blessings?

Luke entered the house, his jaw set in a grim line. "Mom, did Faith fill you in?"

"Yes, dear. How horrible. But I know you'll take care of everything."

"I appreciate your confidence," Luke stated and motioned for Faith to follow him into the hall.

Faith rose and met him in the hall. "I'm sorry I've brought all this trouble here," she said, before he had a chance to speak.

His expression softened. "Don't be. I'm glad you're here."

Thinking of what Dottie had said, with her heart in her throat, she asked, "Why?"

"You're safe and my mom's happy."

That wasn't enough. Disappointment tightened a knot in her chest and must have shown on her face.

He held up a hand. "Look. Right now is complicated."

She tried to smile. "I know."

"I'm going to do what I can to put an end to this situation."

She tensed. "What do you mean?"

"Palmero wants to play a game of cat and mouse, I'll give him a game of cat and mouse."

Fighting back the anxious ripple skating across

her skin, she put a hand on his arm. "Please don't do anything rash. I couldn't stand it if something happened to you."

He touched her cheek. "Nothing's going to happen to me. Or you."

She pressed her cheek into his palm, so desperately wanting to believe him. But her heart warned her he shouldn't promise things he had no control over.

Later that night, Luke left his office to find Faith sitting on the floor of the living room with Brandy. The light from the fire touched her face with its amber glow. Her gaze was fixated on the Christmas tree.

He took a seat on the leather recliner near them. "The tree is beautiful."

A slight smile touched her lips. "When I was a kid, we'd put up a twelve-foot-tall tree in the entryway of my grandparents' house and the staff would decorate it in gold and white ornaments that didn't mean anything. I like this tree so much better. Each ornament has a story to tell of your family."

He'd never thought of that, but she was right. He could look at any one of the dangling doodads and remember a past Christmas. "This will be the first one without my father."

Her gaze held compassion. "But your memories will never disappear."

"True." He leaned forward as a way to put emphasis to his words. "Vinnie is still in New York."

She blinked. "How did you find that out?"

"I called his office."

Her eyes grew big. "You talked to him?"

"I asked his secretary if he was available. She said he was on another line and would I care to hold. I hung up. My intent was to verify his whereabouts, not engage him. Yet."

"But that doesn't mean he didn't hire someone to try to shoot me."

"True. And I'm sure he did. Now, we just have to figure out who. Sisters is a small community but we attract a lot of tourists. Especially with Black Butte and Sunriver resorts in the area. And with Bend, Redmond and La Pine so close—" He shrugged. "That's a lot of territory for someone to hide in."

"Great. That's reassuring."

"It's realistic. I don't want you to attend the Christmas festival at church on Christmas Eve. Leaving the ranch is too chancy."

She pinned him with an intense look. "I'm tired of running. I want to go. If something happens to me, then it was meant to. But I want to go to church on Christmas Eve."

He should have guessed she'd say as much.

Independent, brave. Strong-willed and oh, so appealing.

Whoa! Not going there. Too much was at stake. Stick to business, Campbell. "Sheriff Bane won't like it."

"I don't care."

Her courage and determination revealed a core of steel. This was the woman who'd left a bad situation in order to protect others. A woman fighting to maintain control of her life. "Fine. I'll stick close to you."

Her mouth quirked up at the corners. "I can live with that."

Silence stretched for a moment. A log shifted in the fireplace, letting off a smooth hiss.

"What are the good parts?" she asked.

"The good parts?"

"Of your military career."

For once an easy answer. "My ministry."

Her eyes widened. "You have a ministry? You're a pastor?"

He laughed. "No, I'm not a pastor. I started a Bible fellowship study group in my unit. We began with a few guys, but over the years it's grown. I've been helping the chaplain develop other groups in other units."

He couldn't keep the excitement out of his voice. "I'm hoping to develop a national ministry in all areas of the armed forces. The leaders of the national Promise Keepers are very encouraging. They're giving me good advice and help. I think this will really be a positive undertaking."

"That's very ambitious." Faith turned away. "You must be anxious to get back."

Luke was about to say yes, but hesitated. He wanted to return, to finish what he'd started… He stared at her profile, fighting for control of his heart.

Faith turned to look at him. "What?"

"You are so beautiful," he said truthfully.

"Luke." Her tone scoffed at his words and her gaze dropped to her lap.

"You are."

"I'm glad you think so." She lifted her gaze back to him, her eyes sparkling in the twinkle of lights from the tree. "You're beautiful, too."

He smiled, pleased she thought so, though he couldn't remember anyone ever telling him that before. On impulse, he bent closer, his lips hovering over hers. He heard her sharp intake of breath and felt her lean toward him. Their lips met, warm and yielding. His world narrowed to this particular moment in time.

With Faith in his arms, their lips joined, his heart pulsing, he couldn't decide where he ended and she began. For this one instance, they were one and everything inside of him wanted to hold on to her forever.

Outside, an earsplitting shriek broke the night air, jarring Luke away from Faith's mouth.

No! It wasn't time yet.

Distress and fear drove him to his feet. There hadn't been any of the usual signs.

"What is it?" Faith asked, her voice filled with panic. She clutched at him.

"Lucy." He freed her hands from his shirt. "Stay here."

He ran for the door and vaulted down the porch stairs, nearly colliding with Charles, who'd come running from the barn.

"Something's wrong. Lucy's in labor, but it's gone bad. The vet's not going to make it here in time." Charles's anxiety showed in his tone. Without waiting for a reply, he turned and ran back to the llama barn.

Luke hurried after him. Faith ignored his command and followed.

"What's happening?" Jerry came running down the apartment stairs, his gaze searching for danger. "What's wrong?"

"Lucy's having a difficult birth," Luke explained.

Jerry visibly relaxed and rushed into the barn. "Oh. Okay. What can I do?"

The scene in the barn stole all of her attention. Faith's hand went to her mouth at the sight of the large brown llama lying on her side. The animal's head thrashed about and her swollen belly looked misshapen and painful. Lucy's legs kicked wildly while she tried to right herself to a standing position.

Leo knelt beside Lucy speaking in soothing tones, but his calming words made little difference.

Luke was on his knees beside the animal, his hands assessing the position of the baby. "Charles, towels, blankets, warm water and the first-aid kit. Hurry! We have to help her with this baby now."

Faith jumped out of the way as Charles quickly rushed after the items requested. She took her bottom lip between her teeth, then ventured, "Can I help?"

Without sparing her a glance, Luke gave her instructions. "Get behind her head. Talk to her, try to calm her down. Jerry, steady her flank."

Glad to have some direction, Faith moved and sat behind Lucy's thrashing head. Her hands sought to calm the beast and with gentle ministrations, Lucy's head slowly came to rest on Faith's lap. "There now, you'll be all right soon. Luke will take care of you."

Charles returned, bearing the supplies. Luke glanced up and nodded with his head. "Good. The baby's breech and trying to come backward. Jerry, hold Lucy's legs. Faith, keep talking to her. And watch out because she'll probably start spitting."

"Uh—okay." Unsettled by that bit of information, Faith continued to talk to Lucy. The words were nonsense. Lucy didn't understand, but Faith hoped the llama's wide-eyed stare meant trust.

Concentration etched lines in Luke's forehead. When he put on a pair of rubber gloves, Faith faltered in her one-sided dialogue. Luke met her gaze, tension radiating from his clenched jaw and worried expression.

"We have to turn the baby." He answered her unspoken question.

For a moment, she felt faint at the implications of his words. She looked away and began to sing a lullaby she remembered her mother singing to her when she was a child.

Lucy twitched and bellowed as Luke and Leo worked. Unable to watch, helpless, Faith continued to sing and stroked the llama's head.

Then suddenly, Luke's voice mingled with her own, the deep timbre crooning with sweet words of encouragement.

Lucy's head began to whip around and green spit flew from her mouth. Faith moved back slightly to avoid the spray and gave Luke a harried glance, only to quickly turn away. His arms were buried to his elbow within Lucy's womb and Leo was manipulating from the outside.

Time crawled by, yet for Faith, the world ran on fast forward. Her heart rate accelerated with Lucy's every cry and sweat ran down her temple, but she didn't want to stop caressing the animal to wipe the moisture away.

Suddenly Lucy jerked and struggled to stand. Frightened, Faith scrambled away. Lucy managed to get all four feet under her and hoist herself up.

"Here we go," Luke said, his voice sounding strained.

Chancing another glance toward Luke, Faith's breathing stopped. He had moved with Lucy and now squatted nearly beneath her. Tugging and grunting, he pulled at the baby llama until it slipped from its mother's womb with a swoosh. Lucy collapsed, her body limp and her breathing slow and shallow.

A sense of awe filled Faith. She watched Luke hold the baby close to his chest for a moment with tears in his eyes, then he grabbed at the towels and wiped the baby down. Wrapping a blanket around the newborn, he handed it over to Leo who guided the infant to its mother. Soon the baby was hungrily nursing. Lucy gave an audible sigh.

"Good job, boss," Charles commented as he gathered up the used supplies and then quietly left the barn.

"He's beautiful," Faith whispered.

Luke grinned at her. "He's a she."

Pride and trust swelled within her breast for this

man who'd taken her in and given her a home. "You saved them both, Luke. I knew you could."

In a moment of clarity, love for Luke filled her, overflowing.

But immediately doubts invaded her mind. Could she trust her heart to really know love? Was she responding to the moment and calling it love?

"You helped." The tender look he gave her made her heart pound and a blush worked its way up her neck, the heat flaming her cheeks. Did he feel the same? Was he coming to care for her?

The baby llama pulled away from Lucy and rose on wobbly legs. Faith stared in astonishment as the baby began to walk slowly around, sniffing at her mother. Lucy raised her head and met her offspring's nose.

Fascinated with the bond forming right before her eyes, Faith whispered, "That's so sweet."

"It is sweet."

She shifted her gaze back to him. The moment stretched, their silent communication vibrated in the air.

"I'm naming the baby Faith, so we'll always have something to remember you by," he stated softly.

Her heart twisted.

Nothing could have reminded her more eloquently that her time here was borrowed. He rightly assumed that once the danger passed they'd go their separate ways. Luke didn't love her. What could be more clear?

It was one-sided, this emotional charge she kept feeling. The realization was bitter to take, yet on some level, it was better this way.

Thankfully, she hadn't said the words that would change things between them. The growing closeness she felt now could only be defined as friendship. Nothing more, nothing less.

She tried for a light smile, but could feel the corners of her mouth quiver. "I'll go back to the house. I'm exhausted."

"Thank you for your help tonight." His quiet, somber words echoed off the barn walls.

All she could do was nod and hurry away before the ache in her heart showed on her face.

From the shadows, a man watched Faith hurry inside the house. He could have grabbed her then, but didn't want to chance it, not with so many people roaming about.

His jaw tightened with frustration. He'd thought for sure the bullets would scare her off the ranch where she'd be more vulnerable since Reva's ideas didn't work.

A lot of money had been promised if he could deliver the woman. He needed that money.

In the next day or so, he'd find an opportunity. Soldier man couldn't stay with her around the clock. He glanced at the window that just lit up. Faith's room. Hmm. Maybe a midnight grab?

Naw. Too risky.

There had to be a way to get Faith alone.

"Buck broke through the south pasture fence again. Charles is herding him into the north pasture with the cows," Leo stated when he found Luke in the barn cleaning up after the vet's late-afternoon visit.

Luke sighed. "Ugh, that bull!" Glancing out the barn door at the low sun, they'd be missing dinner tonight. "Well, we best get to it now before it gets too dark. Buck doesn't play well with others."

"I'll go round up Mac and Jerry and get the supplies loaded in the truck."

Luke stepped inside the house to inform Faith he wouldn't be home for dinner. The aromatic scents of tomatoes and spices filled the air. The sight of Faith at the stove, her hair tied back, her cheeks flushed from the heat, made his insides clench. Steeling himself against the attraction ricocheting through him, he said, "Faith."

She jumped and the spoon clattered inside the steaming pot she'd been stirring.

"What's wrong?" she asked, her voice sounding panicky.

"Nothing's wrong." He immediately assured her. "A bull broke through a fence. You and Mom go ahead and eat."

"You're not going to try to fix the fence in the dark, are you?"

He shrugged. "It has to be done. We have a portable floodlight."

"You'll be careful?"

"Always. Lock the door behind me and if you get scared, call me on my cell."

"We'll be fine." She gave him a smile that he was sure meant to inspire confidence.

"I'll leave Brandy with you," he stated. Faith and

his mother would be safe. Deputy Russell was down at the end of the drive. There was no reason to worry. Still, he paused outside the door until he heard the lock slide into place.

Moonlight streamed through the slit in the curtains, the white glow illuminating Faith's path as she paced the kitchen. In the oven she had a plate warming for Luke, but he hadn't returned from fixing the bull-trampled fence. Maybe something happened to him?

No, she couldn't think that way. She was becoming way too attached; to the ranch, Dottie and especially, Luke. Eventually, they would part ways.

When all was said and done, Faith wondered what would become of her. Where would she go? Not back to New York where memories of Vinnie would haunt her, never back there. There wasn't anywhere she wanted to be other than where she was. Already in the short time she'd been in Oregon, she'd made true friends, Dottie, Sally and Matt Turner and of course, Luke.

Her fists clenched in useless frustration. In this house she was accepted for herself, not for her money or her position in society. Here she belonged.

She glanced at the clock. Where was he? The four walls of the kitchen closed in on her. She needed to get outside and breathe some fresh air. She left the house to visit her namesake.

Baby Faith came directly to her, as did Lucy. Both animals nuzzled against her, making her feel wanted and loved.

"Well, at least you love me." Faith knew self-pity was an undesirable quality, but at the moment she felt the need to wallow. Luke didn't love her. She had to accept that.

Faith sang softly to the llamas, her voice clear and bright in the night air. She sang a sad song of love found and love lost.

From behind her, a hand closed over her mouth. Her song turned into a muffled scream.

Close to her ear, a male voice, gloated, "Got you."

Terror roared in her brain. She tried to break free, her elbows driving backward, her legs kicking. An arm snaked around her waist, beneath her rib cage and tightened as she was pulled backward. She twisted and scratched at the hand across her face. Her heels dug into the ground, but she was no match for the man pulling her out of the barn.

From inside the house, Brandy's frantic barks echoed in the quiet of the night. Why hadn't she brought Brandy out with her? *Please, let Dottie look out the window and see what's happening.*

She was slammed up against the side of a dark sedan, parked behind the barn. The door handle jabbed painfully into her hip. The hand at her mouth released. She took a breath to scream, but her air supply was cut off when the man jammed his forearm across her throat, knocking the breath from her.

She heard the sound of pulling tape and then a wide strip of adhesive was slapped over her mouth. Her hands were yanked behind her and taped together. She was pulled away from the car, the door jerked open and she was thrown in. The dome light didn't come on. Faith couldn't make out her attacker's face.

The man captured her feet and taped them together. Then flipped her over so that she landed across the floor of the back seat. A musty-smelling blanket was thrown over her.

A moment later the engine rumbled to life and the car moved slowly forward down the drive, then stopped. Hope flared through her. The hiss of the electric window going down was drowned out by the sudden blare of music from the radio.

The driver had to shout to be heard. "Hey, Deputy."

"Evening. Where you headed?"

"Bend. My mom took a turn for the worse."

Shock jerked through Faith. Mac, the ranch hand with the ill mother? Why was he kidnapping her?

She thumped her tied feet against the floorboards and screamed into the tape across her mouth. She tried to sit up, but she was wedged between the front and back seats at too awkward an angle.

The radio went up a notch. Faith didn't hear the deputy's response before the car began moving again. Then the radio shut off and the roar of the ice-crusted road beneath the car tires reverberated inside Faith's brain along with her pleas to God for help.

TWELVE

"I'll go tell Charles to bring Buck back," Leo stated as they were finishing up with the fence. Puffs of breath visible in the floodlights marked the chilly night air. The ground crunched beneath their feet as they moved about.

"I thought Mac was already doing that," Luke replied, replacing his tools into the back of the Bronco.

Jerry lifted the wooden slats they hadn't needed and carried them to Leo's truck. "I thought he went to get some more nails, but it turned out we didn't need any."

"More nails? I have a ton in here," Luke gestured to the workbox in the back of the Bronco. "When did he leave?"

"Fifteen, twenty minutes ago."

Charles came riding up on a small ATV. "Hey, Buck's not one to be patient. Any chance you all are about done here?"

"Where's Mac?" Leo asked.

Charles shrugged. "I haven't seen Mac since I rode out."

Luke didn't like the uneasy feeling coming over him. "I'm going to head back to the house. You guys finish up here."

"I'll come with you," Jerry said.

Luke didn't want to take the time to argue. He climbed in and drove quickly over the rough, ice-crusted ground back to the ranch. As soon as he pulled up he knew something was wrong. His mother and Brandy were waiting on the back porch.

"She's gone!" his mother exclaimed.

"What happened?" Luke's heart pounded in his head like a hammer hitting a post.

"I don't know. Brandy was barking so wildly. Like she did the other night. I came downstairs and I couldn't find Faith."

"The deputy," Jerry said.

"Go inside and lock the door," Luke instructed his mother. "I'll find her."

To Jerry he said, "I need you to stay and keep an eye out. Let Leo and Charles know what's up when they return."

"Sure thing," Jerry stated.

Luke hesitated, then decided he'd better go armed. He wasn't sure what Mac was up to, or why, but Luke didn't want to go into the situation unprepared. He ran up to his room where he kept a Glock in a small lockbox under his bed. Once in his Bronco, he sped down the drive, the tires slipping. He skidded to a halt at the end of the road. The deputy got out of his car and came over.

"Did you see anyone leave here?" Luke asked, his voice sharp.

The deputy nodded. "Yeah, Mac left just a bit ago. Said his mother took a turn for the worse, so he was going to Bend to see her. What's up?"

The news slammed into Luke's chest like mortar fire. How could he have been so blind? "Call the sheriff. Give him a description of Mac's car. I think he kidnapped Faith."

Without a word, the deputy ran back to his cruiser. Luke turned out onto the road, his mind frantically going over the options.

If he was going to try to get her out of the state, he'd either drive or take a private plane. Driving was too risky. He'd know the police would be looking for him. Roberts Field Airport in Redmond was about fifteen miles outside of Bend, which had smaller commercial planes. Bend Municipal Airport just northeast of Bend handled Lears and more private planes. The closest major airport was in Portland. Mac wouldn't take her to a major one. Too many people. Of the other two, Luke had a fifty-fifty shot. He chose Bend Municipal.

Luke drove as fast as the slick roads allowed. He prayed he'd find Faith before it was too late.

The shrill ring of a phone jolted through Faith. Already tense muscles tightened even more. Her body ached from being on the floor of the car. She strained to hear Mac as he answered.

"Yeah, I got her. We're about ten minutes out. What? You never said anything about that. Let me check."

The car slowed, the sound of loose road debris

hit the underbelly of the car as they came to a stop, the engine left to idle. The blanket was pulled off of her. Mac twisted around in his seat and loomed over Faith. Her body went rigid. Her heart pounded fiercely against her rib cage.

Mac grabbed her by the throat, and rubbed his hand along her neck and collarbone before releasing her.

Relief rushed through her veins, making the world spin.

"No," Mac said once he was back in his seat. He put the car in gear. "Too bad, dude. That's your problem. You didn't say I had to get anything else. I've got the woman and you've better have the hundred grand."

So a hundred-thousand dollars bought Mac's betrayal. Disgusting.

Faith closed her eyes and continued to pray.

Luke's Bronco skidded to a stop in the parking lot of the airport. He bolted from the vehicle. A blanket of powdery snow covered everything but the black tarmac where a small twin-engine plane prepared to take off.

Luke's gaze searched the airport and landed on a Cessna on the far side of the tarmac.

Mac's sedan was parked by the plane. Mac emerged from the driver's side and opened the back door. He leaned in and seemed to be struggling with something. Mac's fist rose then slammed down before he dragged something out on to the ground. A body.

Luke's heart jumped to his throat. Faith!

Automatically shifting into military mode, he took off at a dead run.

Mac had picked up Faith's bound form and hoisted her into the cabin of the plane.

The pilot gestured wildly toward Luke. Mac jumped in and slammed the door closed. The rotators whirled, the sound rushing into Luke's ears as he reached the side of the plane. He yanked at the door handle. It wouldn't budge. He could see Mac urging the pilot on. The plane started to move.

Luke drew his weapon and ran hard to get in front of the plane. He aimed at the wheels and fired.

The plane slowed and limped off the runway into the thick snow. Luke rushed to the plane.

The pilot jumped out his hands in the air. "Hey, man. Don't shoot me."

"On the ground, hands behind your head," Luke commanded. "Mac! Come out. Keep your hands up."

For a second, he thought Mac was going to comply, but then he dived for the door on the other side of the cabin. He hit the ground running.

Luke found Faith curled up on the floor behind the plane's front seats. A large nasty bruise dominated one cheek. Pulse-pounding dread drowned out the sounds of everything but the faint hiss of her breath. She was alive, but he'd failed to protect her. He'd never forgive himself.

He gathered her up and carried her from the plane. He took her to the sedan and laid her gently on the seat. Taking out a pocketknife, Luke cut the tape binding her arms and legs. Carefully, he removed the tape across her mouth. She didn't so much as flinch.

He pulled out his cell phone and dialed 9-1-1. He told the operator what was needed and hung up.

"Please, God. Oh, please." He stroked Faith's hair back from her face. "Faith. Come on, Faith."

Helplessness, heavy and dark centered in the middle of his chest. All his battlefield first-aid training was useless in this situation. His heart hurt so badly he thought he'd be ripped in two. He should have protected her better.

Sirens filled the night air as the local police, sheriff and an ambulance descended on the tarmac.

Within moments a paramedic crouched beside the open door. "Sir, we need to help her."

Luke let the paramedics move her to the ground where they assessed her condition.

"You okay?" Sheriff Bane asked as he came to stand beside Luke.

"Me, yeah." His gaze stayed riveted to Faith. "Mac got away."

"We got him."

Rage twisted in Luke's gut. "I want to talk to him."

"I'm sure you do," Bane stated. "But we'll follow procedure."

Luke wanted nothing more than to put his hands around Mac's throat and squeeze. "How did Palmero get to Mac?"

"When I know something, I'll let you know."

The paramedics lifted Faith onto a gurney and slid it into the ambulance.

"I'll be at the hospital," Luke told the sheriff before jumping into the ambulance.

He took Faith's hand and leaned close to her ear. "You're going to be all right. I promise."

The ride to the hospital seemed to take forever. Faith lay so still and pale. She looked okay, except for the purple mark on her face where Mac had punched her. That awful reminder of how Luke had failed to protect her made him want to retch.

At the hospital, Faith was whisked away by the medical personnel. Luke paced the sterile waiting room and refused to consider that she wouldn't be all right.

"Are you Luke?" an older man, wearing a white doctor's coat, asked as he approached.

"Yes. Faith?"

"She has a concussion and is a bit disoriented, which isn't uncommon after head trauma. There was no sexual assault."

Luke swallowed back bile at the very idea that she could have been raped.

"She's asking for you."

A wave of relief crashed over Luke. "Please, lead the way."

Faith's face brightened when he walked in the room. The dark bruise on her face tore at his conscience. He rushed to her side. "It's good to see your smile."

"I'm just thankful to be out of that car. What happened to Mac?"

"He's been taken into custody." Luke held her

soft hand. "Don't worry about him. He's no longer a threat to you."

"That doesn't mean there won't be someone else. Vinnie got so close."

A cold knot formed in Luke's gut. "Yes. He won't again," Luke vowed. "I'm sorry I failed to protect you."

"Oh, no, Luke. This isn't your fault. You had no way of knowing."

He shook his head. "I should have been more careful."

"Please, don't feel guilty." Her eyebrows drew together. "Mac was getting a hundred-thousand dollars for me. But he got a call and it sounded like he was supposed to get something else."

"Like what?"

She sighed. "I don't know. It all seems so surreal."

"Then don't think anymore about it." He squeezed her hand. "For now, you need to concentrate on getting better."

"The doctor said I'll have to stay the night."

"I'll stay with you."

She squeezed his hand. "No. You need to go home and be with your mom. I'll be safe enough here. I'm just going to sleep anyway."

She would be safe, but still Luke didn't want to let her out of his sight.

"Please, go, Luke. I'll be fine."

"I'll have the sheriff post a man outside your door."

"If that makes you feel better," she said softly.

"It will. I'll be back first thing tomorrow."

She smiled and let her eyes drift shut. Luke kissed the back of her hand before quietly leaving the room.

He sagged against the wall outside of her door. He'd never been more afraid in his whole life than he had been in the last hour. So much for not becoming attached to his employee.

He called his mother and told her that Faith was well and that he'd be home soon. But first he had a stop to make.

At the sheriff's station, Luke was led into the sheriff's office to wait. The room was small but functional, with a desk, computer workstation and a bookshelf full of manuals and such. Luke ignored the guest chairs and stood by the window to stare at the dark sky.

"Thank You, Lord, for giving her back to me. I won't let You down again," he whispered.

The door behind him opened. Sheriff Bane walked in, his gaze disapproving. "I said I'd call when I had information to give you."

"What has he said?"

"Nothing." Bane sat behind his desk. "He lawyered up."

"Let me see him." Luke clenched his fist. "I'll make him talk."

Bane gave him a droll stare. "And throw the arrest out the window? I don't think so."

"Did you at least confirm Palmero hired him?"

"Like I said, he's not talking."

Anger boiled in Luke's veins. "Palmero's behind this."

Bane nodded. "From what you've told me, I agree. But proving it will be hard unless Mac cooperates."

"What about the pilot?"

"He claims he was just hired by Mac."

"Where was he supposed to take them?"

"His flight plan said Boise."

"Then Mac must have had other transportation arrangements there," Luke said.

"We're looking into it." Bane stood and came around the desk. "I promise you, I'll let you know the minute I have anything concrete. But for now, the best thing for you to do is take care of your family."

His family. Faith had become part of his family these past weeks. The certainty sent his heart reeling with awe and tenderness.

"Can you put someone at the hospital to protect Faith?"

"Already ahead of you on that one. Deputy Russell should be there now."

Luke left the sheriff's station and headed back to the ranch. Tomorrow he'd bring Faith home.

And he wouldn't ever let her go.

The ranch came into view. Sprawling and beautiful, just like the first time she'd laid eyes on the Circle C. A sense of coming home infused Faith as Luke turned onto the gravel drive. For the moment she wasn't going to fight the attachment or the sense of well-being. For now she'd soak it up.

The front door opened and Brandy shot out like a cannon and bounded down the porch stairs, barking happily. Dottie came to stand by the railing, a welcoming smile on her face. The mother Faith had so often longed for.

Luke parked and came around to open the passenger door. Brandy practically knocked him over in her effort to greet Faith. She accepted the dog's sloppy love before Luke nudged Brandy aside and held out his hand. Faith grasped his big strong hand and let him lead her to the house. There was nothing sisterly about her reaction to Luke. Her heart sped up and her senses fired little fissures of heat over her skin.

He didn't let go until they were on the porch. His mother gave her a fierce embrace.

"I was so scared," Dottie said with a sniff.

"Me, too," Faith answered.

Once inside the house, Dottie led Faith to the couch. "Here now. Let me get you some soothing tea," Dottie cooed and bustled into the kitchen.

Relaxing back into the cushions, Faith closed her eyes, aware of Luke hovering nearby.

"Would you like to go to your room?" Luke asked.

"I'm fine here," she replied. "Shouldn't you and Dottie head to the festival? It's Christmas Eve, after all."

"We're not going anywhere," he stated and sat beside her, his warmth reaching her without his even touching her. She opened her eyes to study him. His hair had grown since that first day and now showed signs of curling. The brightness of his blue eyes held her. She tried to decipher what emotions lurked in those liquid pools but couldn't. Maybe she was too tired and overwhelmed, or maybe he was just that good at hiding his feelings.

"Are you sure you're okay?" he asked.

"The doctor said I was." She reached out for his hand. "Thank you for what you did."

His fingers closed over hers, warm and reassuring.

"Here we go." Dottie returned, carrying a tray with a teapot and three cups. She set it on the coffee table and poured them each a cup.

Faith didn't want to release her hold on Luke to take the offered cup, but had no choice. She held the warm mug in her hands and tried to allow calm to seep through her.

Dottie sat in her recliner. "Luke, honey, I hate to ask, but would you be willing to take the pies we made to the church by noon? I called Sally and asked her to let them know we wouldn't be coming today, but they could still use the pies."

Luke inclined his head. "I'll see if Leo can drive them out."

"That would work."

"You two can still go," Faith said. She didn't like that her situation was preventing Dottie from doing something she'd been looking forward to.

"Nonsense." Dottie waved away her words. "Why don't we see if there's a Christmas movie on TV." Dottie picked up the remote. "I just love that one with Jimmy Stewart and the angel."

Thinking she'd found two earthly angels of her own right here, Faith smiled. "I do, too."

Luke stood. "As much as I want to join you, I have some calls to make."

Faith watched Luke stride from the room, taking

his warmth and energy with him. She set her mug down and settled back as Dottie flipped through the channels.

For a moment Faith stared at the television, the flicker of shows hypnotic. Sleepiness overtook her. Her eyelids drooped. The doctor said she should rest, that her head would hurt for a while but she would recover.

Recover enough to leave.

But deep inside, she knew her heart would never recover once she left Luke behind.

Luke sat at his desk and waited on hold while the operator connected him to Roger's direct line.

"Tumble," Rog answered, his drawl unmistakable.

"Rog, it's Luke."

"Hey, how ya doing?"

"I've been better," Luke replied, then told Roger all that had happened.

Roger whistled. "You have had a lot going on. How can I help?"

"I don't know that you can. I wanted to check on that paperwork."

"It's coming your way. I have good news on another front. George Peterson has stepped up to the plate and is doing a great job leading the fellowship studies. He's even talked with the guys from the Promise Keepers and is moving forward with your plans. I figured you'd be okay with it."

Luke sat back. He hadn't expected that news. And he wasn't sure how he felt about it. Regardless, he said, "That's fine. Hey, I'll give you a call later. I've got to go."

"Sure. Let me know if I can do anything."

"I will."

Luke stared out of his office window at the mountain range and tried to make sense of all that was happening. He couldn't.

His old life didn't seem to be waiting for him.

He should be grateful that someone was following through with his plans but...

He fought back hard feelings. He'd developed the program; he'd spent countless hours building the Bible study. He should be the one to see it grow, to see his plans fulfilled. He shook his head, disappointed in himself for feeling...jealous.

It wasn't his plan or his Bible study. It belonged to God. He'd started it, yes, but because God had called him to it. And now Luke wanted the glory?

He hung his head in remorse. "Forgive me, Lord."

Taking a deep cleansing breath, he scrubbed his hands over his face. Now what? What plan did the Lord have for him now?

The phone rang, jarring him out of his thoughts. "Hello?"

"Matt here. Sally said you all weren't coming into town today. I was hoping to talk with you. I have a proposition for you."

"Can it wait until next week?"

"Not really. I just need an hour. Could we meet at the diner?"

Luke drummed his fingers on the desk. He was going to have Leo run into town, but...he'd just make sure the guys kept a vigilant eye out. "Yeah, that'd be fine. I have to take some pies over to the church at noon, so how about we meet at twelve-fifteen?"

"Sounds great. Thanks," Matt said and hung up.

When Luke entered the living room, Faith was fast asleep on the couch. She looked so vulnerable and sweet. His heart spasmed with a wellspring of tenderness. He grabbed a blanket from the closet and laid it over her.

He whispered to his mother, "I'll be taking the pies into town."

At the flicker of surprise in his mother's eyes, he added, "I'll make sure Leo knows I won't be here. He'll look out for you two."

Dottie patted his hand with approval.

Luke found his most trusted hand with the baby llama.

"Hi, boss," Leo greeted him.

"Hey, I have to run into town. Can you keep an eye out?"

"Sure, thing. Glad to see that young girl back safe and sound." He shook his head. "Still can't get over Mac being so rotten. Makes for a strange Christmas."

Luke gave a dry laugh. Very strange indeed.

After talking some more with Leo, Luke left the barn to load the pies in the back of his truck. Brandy whined when he wouldn't let her in the back with the food.

"You'd eat them for sure, girl."

She barked as if to deny the accusation.

When Luke opened the driver's side door, Brandy

leaped inside and sat in the passenger seat. Her normal spot when he took her with him.

"Hey, girl, not this trip," Luke said. "Come on out of there."

Brandy laid down in response. Her paws hung over the edge of the seat and her tail thumped against the door. She stared at him with big pleading eyes.

"Stubborn dog," Luke muttered and climbed in.

After dropping off the pies, he parked outside the diner, cracked the window for Brandy and headed for the door.

He sat at the counter and immediately Ethel set down a steaming cup of coffee. Nodding his thanks, he sipped from the strong brew, aware of the waitress's steady regard. Raising his brows, he asked, "Is something the matter?"

"Well, I don't rightly know. That investigator fellow was back here this morning and he had a friend with him this time."

Coffee sloshed onto the counter and Luke set the cup down. A horrified feeling settled over him, making his voice rough. "What did his friend look like?"

Ethel tapped a finger against her chin. "Well, now. Thin, average height, sort of slick. You know, city type."

Pressure throbbed behind his eyes. Luke's hands fisted on the countertop. "What did they want?"

Ethel narrowed her eyes. "I'm not sure, but Reva was cozying up to them, and if you ask me, that bodes trouble for sure."

Apprehension slithered across Luke's flesh, causing bumps to pucker his skin. He stood. "How long ago were they here? Any idea where they were headed?" Luke couldn't keep the urgency from his tone.

Ethel's worried expression matched what Luke felt. "They left an hour ago. Didn't hear where they were going. But Reva's working at the General Store now. You could go ask her."

"Call Sheriff Bane and tell him to send a car to the ranch." He was practically out the door before he thought to call over his shoulder, "Thanks, Ethel."

"Anytime, honey," she said as the door closed behind him.

The General Store, so called because it carried everything from groceries to hardware, sat a block down Main Street. Luke entered the store and headed straight for Reva. She stopped stacking the cans of soup to smile at him.

Luke backed her into a corner and growled, "All right, Reva. What kind of game are you playing?"

Her smile faltered for a brief second. "I—I don't know what you're talking about."

"Don't toy with me, Reva. I know you were talking with that private investigator. What did you tell him?"

"Why, just the truth." She stepped around him and continued stocking the shelves.

Luke clenched his fists in an effort to control his rising temper. "And what truth would that be?"

"Oh, just that Mr. Palmero's *wife* could be found at the Circle C."

Wanting nothing more than to shake her until her

tongue rattled loose, he ground out between gritted teeth, "Do you know what you've done?"

She stared at him, the picture of innocence. "I just steered a husband to his wife."

"She's his ex-wife, Reva. And what you've done is put Faith and my mother in danger."

Anger and fear raged in large waves to the fore-front of his consciousness. He'd promised to protect Faith and again he wasn't there when she needed him. "Are they on their way there now?"

"I suppose." Reva's brows drew together. "You don't really think he'd harm them, do you?"

"Your concern is a little late." Disgusted, he whirled away, but was stopped short by Reva's voice.

"If only she'd gotten scared and left, this wouldn't be happening and you'd still be mine."

Without turning back around, he asked, "What do you mean?"

"If she would have just run like she was supposed to. I mean, how stupid to stay when she was warned to leave!" Bitterness cloaked her words, making her sound petulant and petty.

He turned to stare at her. "The note and the phone calls. Those were your doing. You lied to the sheriff when he asked you about them."

"I was losing you, Luke. I had to do something. Those weren't my ideas, they were Mac's." She stepped toward him, her hand reached out beseech-ingly.

Luke shook his head in disbelief. He'd never have thought her capable of such treachery. "You never had me, Reva."

Running from the store, Luke headed for his truck. Speeding through town, he picked up his cell phone and dialed the house, but the phone only rang and rang. Fear and anger took turns seizing his gut. Brandy barked wildly, as if urging him to go faster.

Dear God, I can't lose Faith. I'm begging You, protect my family. Don't let me be too late.

If anything happened to his family, he didn't know if he'd be able to stop himself from killing Vince Palmero.

THIRTEEN

Bundled against the crisp air, Faith stared in silent contemplation, her gaze taking in the snow-covered peaks and trees off in the distance but not really appreciating their beauty. From the back porch of the Circle C, the mountains looked as if she could reach out and touch them.

Her fingers fumbled with a ball of yarn and knitting needles as her mind tried to grasp what Dottie was saying from her seat beside her, but all she could concentrate on was not thinking about the official-looking letter lying on top of a stack of mail that sat on the little side table.

The seal said U.S. Army and Faith's stomach churned. Was Luke being sent on a mission? Would he go, when he'd promised to stay until her problems were resolved?

Resolved? Ha! She doubted she'd ever see resolution. She'd always have the threat of Vinnie hanging over her head. He knew his way around the law too well.

Picking up the ball of yarn from her lap, she went

back to practicing the stitches Dottie had shown her. She was trying to make a cap for Luke to give him tomorrow on Christmas Day. But she kept having to back stitch because she couldn't concentrate.

"Well, well, well. If this isn't a sight to remember. My dear little wife turned country bumpkin."

The ball of yarn fell from her hands and rolled across the porch and disappeared off the side.

Faith looked up and the all-too-familiar sneer jarred her to the very core. Vinnie. Her worst nightmare had come true.

Under his long trench coat, his silk designer suit, usually sharply pressed, showed creases. His jet-black hair, normally slicked back with gel, fell forward in stringy strands. The prized Italian loafers were scuffed. She'd never seen him so disheveled or so desperate.

"Who are you?" Dottie demanded to know, her eyebrows slammed together in a frown.

Ignoring Dottie, Vinnie stepped onto the porch, his voice dripping with sarcasm. "No tearful greeting, Faith? I thought for sure you'd be ready to come home by now. This little rebellion of yours is getting quite tedious."

Desperate to avoid the inevitable, Faith looked at Dottie and tried to tell her with her eyes not to antagonize him. The older woman's narrowed gaze sent fresh shivers of alarm down Faith's spine. Where were Leo and the other hands?

A fierce countenance replaced Dottie's usually mild demeanor. It reminded Faith of a mama bear defending her cubs. "You're not wanted here. Leave this instant or I'll call the police."

Faith laid a hand on Dottie's sleeve and shook her head.

"Oh, I don't think you'll be calling anyone," Vinnie gloated.

Dottie's eyes widened and Faith turned to find herself staring down the barrel of a gun. Swallowing, Faith mustered all her bravado. The need to protect Dottie overcoming any tendency towards cowering, she met Vinnie's gaze and held it without wincing.

His dark eyes danced with glee and his thin lips spread into a feral grin, making Faith's stomach lurch.

"Put the gun away, Vinnie. You don't need that." Her voice trembled ever-so-slightly, giving away her inner turmoil. She wished Luke hadn't gone into town. But then again, if he were here, he'd be in danger, too.

Anger burned hot in Vinnie's eyes. "No one betrays me and gets away with it. Come on, Faith. Get your things and let's go."

Vinnie motioned for her to get up.

"Wh—what right do you have to order her about like that? We're not alone here," Dottie piped up, her voice angry. Yet fear underlined each word.

Annoyance narrowed his gaze on Dottie and he swung the gun toward her. "You mean the two men in the barn? They've been taken care of."

Heartsick by the implication of his words, Faith's stomach convulsed. She had to stay strong and not let her fear show. Wanting to bring his attention back to her, Faith stated quickly, "We are no longer married. I don't belong to you."

His attention once again zeroed in on Faith. Possessiveness lit his black eyes with a feral gleam. "You do belong to me."

From inside the house the phone rang. Each ring stretched Faith's nerves.

She took a deep breath, drawing on strength she'd learned from Luke. "No, I don't."

"What?!" His face turned a frightening shade of red and the vein at his temple pulsed into a squiggly, purple line.

"You heard me. I want you to leave." Her voice wavered and she watched his face contort with rage.

Cursing graphically, he stepped threateningly closer, the gun raised and pointed at her chest. "You've made me chase you all the way across the country, forced me to spend good money on flunkies, made a fool of me."

"Leave, Vinnie," Faith repeated, her bravado rapidly retreating, replaced by a gnawing fear. He was unpredictable. She shouldn't push too hard.

"Oh, no, no, no. I'm not leaving here without you. You've caused me too much trouble, Faith, for me to let you go." The black of his eyes took on a sinister gleam, the centers hollow, with no sign of a soul.

"She's not going anywhere with you. My son will be back any second and he won't let you take her away." Dottie sounded so sure, so confident. Her belief in her son rang in every syllable.

For a brief moment, Vinnie's gaze narrowed in speculation on Dottie, then swung back to Faith. His lips spread into a sadistic grin. "If you don't want this old woman to die, you'll pack your things and leave with me now."

Icy talons of fear gripped her heart. She knew he'd shoot Dottie and walk away without any remorse.

"Don't—please don't do this." Faith stood and placed herself in front of Dottie, using herself as a shield for Luke's mother.

Fury consumed his demeanor. His face twisted and he lunged for Faith, knocking over the small table and kicking aside the chair she'd been sitting in. Faith raised her hands to ward him off, dreading the violence to come, but she resolved to protect Dottie. At any cost.

Vinnie's thin hand closed around her neck and sent her backward with a hard shove. She landed with a painful thud in the chair Dottie had just barely vacated. Faith twisted around and caught a glimpse of the older woman—moving faster than she thought possible—disappearing inside the house. She prayed she'd call the police and not come back out.

The cold metal of the gun pressing into her temple brought Faith's gaze back to Vinnie. His fingers dug into her neck and he said in a harsh rasp, "You're mine, Faith. I'll destroy this place and everyone in it, do you hear me?"

His grip tightened, choking her, and she could only nod as she gasped for breath. Darkness threatened to overtake her, but she fought the blackness. She had to stop him. She couldn't let him hurt the Campbells. Praying the police were now on their way, she knew what to do. It'd always worked before. She forced the words out. "I—I'm s-sorry."

The pressure on her neck eased slightly. Vinnie cocked his head and stared at her as if she were a cockroach he'd like to squash.

Heart rebelling against the scene they were about to play out, Faith whispered again the hated words that had saved her many times during her marriage. "I'm—sorry." She knew that to him those two little words meant she was wrong and he was right.

Leaning in closer, his breath hot and sticky against her cheek, he whispered, "I can't hear you."

Desperate anger helped her draw strength from past experience and forced her voice to a louder octave, "I'm sorry."

"Ah, that's better. But what are you sorry for, Faith?"

Briefly she closed her eyes, hating him for finding her, hating herself for having been dumb enough to marry him in the first place. "For—running—away," she ground out.

Abruptly, he pushed away from her and stood, his feet braced apart, the gun still aimed at her. "Tell me," he barked.

She knew the drill. Everything inside her objected, but it was what she had to do. "I—shouldn't have run away from you. You're—you're wonderful, Vinnie, you're everything a girl could ask for. I was—was a fool not to see that. You were there when I had no one and—and I will always be—grateful to you."

With lightning speed, his hand shot out and

grabbed the front of her shirt, yanking her to him. "I don't believe you. I think you like it here."

Desperation clawed at her, this wasn't the way it was supposed to go. Her stomach knotted in fear. "No, no—I—I don't."

"You're lying to me, Faith. I don't like it when you lie. You know how angry that makes me."

Remembering his displeasure, the fear and humiliations that went with it, she cringed. "Yes. Yes, I know."

"Let's go." He grabbed her arm and dragged her toward the porch stairs.

Mind working frantically to get past the overwhelming fear, she latched on to one thought, *stall him*. "Wait," she screamed.

He ignored her and gave a vicious yank. She stumbled, going down hard on her knees. Pain exploded up her legs and wood splintered into her palms as she tried to break her fall.

"Get up," Vinnie yelled.

Faith looked up and saw his raised fist. Reacting instinctively, she scrambled away. Behind her she heard his frustrated curse and looked back to see him stalking menacingly toward her.

Panic gripped her. Keep talking, she told herself. "V-Vinnie," her voice came out a croak, so she tried again. "Vinnie, l-listen to me. You're wrong, I don't like it here." The lie nearly made her retch.

He continued toward her.

Beyond desperate now, she elaborated on the lies. "I—I don't belong on a ranch, I see that now. I belong in New York with you. This hick town can't compare with the excitement of the city and—and these cowpoke people mean nothing to me."

She held her breath as Vinnie stopped and stared at her, mentally gauging her words. She could tell he wasn't convinced, but she'd gained time.

Slowly, she stood and continued, the lies bitter on her tongue. "I—I love you Vinnie. It's al-always been you, you know that. And you love me. You're coming here proves it. I guess I—just needed to have this show of affection to realize how—much."

The subtle change in his expression told her the words were starting to work. He was getting wrapped up in the lies. Dizzy with relief, she continued, hoping to keep him distracted long enough for the sheriff to arrive. "Don't you know? I'd be nothing without you. I really am sorry for causing you so much trouble, though you hired some good detectives. That was very smart of you. You're so smart, Vinnie."

His chest puffed up at the praise. "Yes, I am."

"Of course you are." Bile rose in her throat at the awful sickness of it all.

From her peripheral vision, Faith saw a movement at the stairs. She turned slightly and widened her eyes at the sight of Luke stepping up on the porch. Quickly looking back at Vinnie, she hoped he hadn't followed her gaze with his own.

But he had. The pit of her stomach dropped to see him whirl away from her and raise the gun. "You're a dead man," he shouted.

Faith reacted. Throwing herself at Vinnie, she used her fingers to claw at the gun in his hand. He shoved her away from him with a hand to her chest, sending her into the wall with jarring force.

Luke raised his hands in supplication, his expression neutral. Faith watched in horror, not believing Luke would stand there like an open target. Almost as if he dared Vinnie to shoot.

"Are you a cop?" Vinnie asked, sneering.

Luke shook his head. "No, this is my ranch."

"So, you're the wife-stealer. I ought to shoot you right now and be done with you."

Faith struggled to keep from crying out.

Luke shrugged. "You could. But there's no need. You can have her. I'm done with her. You heard her, she loves you. How can I fight that?" Luke inched forward, so slowly and carefully the movement was hardly noticeable.

Faith's mouth dropped open. He couldn't possibly believe the things she'd said to Vinnie, could he? Or had he figured out the sick game she was forced to play?

"You're right, she does love me," Vinnie postulated, his hawklike features settling into a smug expression. "Come on, Faith, we're leaving." Vinnie held out one hand while the other still aimed the gun at Luke's chest.

Faith stared at Vinnie's outstretched hand and then swung her gaze to Luke, who stared back at her, his blue eyes cold and remote. His stance was almost casual, as if they were doing no more than talking about the weather. How could he be so relaxed?

"Go on, Faith, your husband wants you to leave." Luke's words sliced a gaping hole into Faith's heart. I don't want to leave you, she wanted to scream.

Faith stepped forward, but refused Vinnie's hand. She heard his sound of disapproval, but ignored him. Holding her head high, knowing she'd escape again the first chance she got, she marched in front of Vinnie toward the porch stairs. Tears gathered in her eyes as she passed Luke, but she forced her gaze straight ahead.

Two steps down she heard a noise. She turned back in time to see Luke launch himself at Vinnie. The agility and grace of Luke's body as he struck out amazed her. The rapid-fire movements of Luke's limbs connected with Vinnie's wiry frame, causing a yelp of pain.

She sagged against the railing in overwhelming relief. Luke wasn't going to let Vinnie take her. He was living up to his promise. She felt shame for doubting him. Vinnie turned the gun toward Luke and in a blood-pounding moment her elation turned to terror. She cried, "Nooo."

Unbelievably, Luke stepped in closer, his hands closing around the barrel of the gun. The two men moved in unison, their chests close together as they fell to the porch floor.

Faith covered her mouth with her hands. Fear for Luke washed over her in giant waves, making her nauseous.

The loud retort of the gun split the air, the acrid smell of gun powder burning Faith's nostrils. Shudders ripped through her body at the thought that she might have lost Luke to Vinnie's gun.

Her heart stopped beating. *Please, God.* Neither man moved for what seemed an eternity, then suddenly Luke rolled away and stood. In his hand he held the gun. Faith whimpered in relief. *Thank You.*

She rushed to his side as he bent to check Vinnie's pulse. "Is he—?"

"He's alive," Luke stated and met her gaze.

"Drop the gun."

Startled, Faith jerked her gaze around to find the source of the command as Luke's arm came around her waist. Three men stood near the side of the house. Two held guns aimed at them. Both men were dressed in long trench coats and shiny dress shoes. Faith blinked as her mind registered the smaller man without a weapon. He wore jeans, a leather bomber jacket and his dark hair fell forward over his brown eyes. "Anthony?"

"I said drop the gun," the man on the right barked.

Luke laid the gun on the ground and slowly rose, his arm pulling her behind him. "You know these men?" Luke asked over his shoulder to her.

"Yes. No. I mean—Anthony is Vinnie's brother." She tried to step forward, but Luke held her still, his body protecting her. "What's going on?"

The bigger of the two men shoved Anthony forward and he stumbled to a halt. "Sorry, Faith. I never meant to drag you into this."

"Drag me into what?"

"Enough chitchat," the older of the other two men stepped forward. His demeanor made it obvious he was in charge. "Get it."

Anthony grimaced. "Faith, I need your prayer-box necklace."

"What? Why?" She resisted the urge to reach inside her shirt collar and finger the box.

"I wrote down a number on the back of the prayer. I need that number," Anthony explained, his gaze showing desperation.

"So that's what you were doing in my room." She remembered the day she'd walked in to the bedroom that she'd shared with Vinnie a week before she left. Anthony had been going through her jewelry. She'd figured he'd swiped something to pawn for money to support his gambling habit, but nothing had been missing.

"I need that number or they're going to kill me," Anthony pleaded.

"How do you know that once you give it to them, they won't kill you, and us, anyway?" Luke demanded harshly.

"You don't," the older man stated. His ruddy complexion grew redder with the cold air. "Now get it. I'm freezing here."

"Faith, please. Just do as they ask. Where is it? Inside?" Anthony stepped closer.

"What's the number to?" Luke asked.

"Now if we told you that, we'd really have to kill you," the younger man quipped.

"Shut up, Junior," the older man barked. "Just get the number. I'm running out of patience."

The slight squeak of the porch door sounded seconds before the loud bang of a shotgun. Faith yelped, Anthony dove to the ground with his arms covering his head, the two men swung their guns toward the house and Luke bent to grab the gun from the ground.

Dottie, looking fierce holding a twelve-gauge shotgun aimed at the chest of the older man, moved to the top of the stairs. "Throw your guns on the ground or you'll take one in the chest."

The older man lifted his hands, his gun aimed in the air. "Now, listen here, I just want what's mine."

"You heard the lady, put down your weapons." Sheriff Bane came from around the house, a gun in his hand, as well.

Faith clutched Luke's arm, feeling like she'd somehow been plopped down in the middle of some gangster movie. The distant wail of a siren grew louder, bringing hope of an end to this daylight nightmare.

The older man swore and dropped his gun. The big guy did as his boss. Within moments, the place was swarming with uniformed police officers and men in navy vests with the letters FBI emblazoned across them in bright yellow. Luke helped Faith to the porch, where he took the shotgun from his mother before going to talk with the sheriff.

Faith watched the activity with numb detachment. The two strangers and Anthony were cuffed and put into a cruiser. The private investigator was also apprehended. Leo and Charles had been found tied up in the barn. Vinnie only had a leg wound. Paramedics worked to stop the bleeding.

Unsure how she felt about Vinnie surviving, Faith clenched her hands together. On the one hand she was grateful Luke wasn't responsible for a death.

Yet, with Vinnie alive, her nightmare still lived on. She knew he wouldn't stay in jail forever and then he'd come looking for her again.

She dug out the prayer box from inside the collar of her shirt. Carefully, she opened the lid and pulled out the rolled paper. She stared at the numbers across the back. What were they to? She hurried to where the FBI agent who seemed to be in charge stood giving orders.

"Excuse me," she said as she approached.

"Ma'am," he responded. "Agent Tanner at your service. Can I help you?"

"Yes, sir." She held out the paper. "This is what the men were looking for. Do you know what it is?"

Luke stepped close but didn't touch her. She wished he'd put his arm around her, she needed his solid strength.

"Yes, ma'am. This is a numbered bank account. Mr. Fernando and his associates run a gambling and drug operation in Miami. Hopefully, this will be enough to put them away for a long time."

"How did you know they were here?"

He lowered his voice. "We have a man on the inside of the operation."

"What does Vinnie have to do with any of this?" she asked.

"From what Mr. Campbell, here, tells me, your ex-husband was stalking you. Other than a means for Fernando to find you, Vinnie wasn't involved with the operation. But he will be dealt with on the stalking issue. Now if you'll excuse me."

Agent Tanner left, taking the two men from

Miami and Anthony with him. Luke went to talk with the sheriff.

Needing something to do, Faith righted the chairs and table. Beneath her feet, she heard the crunch of paper and saw the mail scattered about.

Bending down, she began to pick up the pieces of paper and froze as her hand closed around the official-looking envelope. Sadness gathered in her heart. She knew she had to give the letter to Luke.

Her gaze settled on him. He bent down close to where Vinnie was stretched out on a gurney. She frowned. What could he be saying to Vinnie? The ambulance attendants stood a good distance away, leaving Luke alone with the wounded man.

She could see the same hardness in Luke's face that she'd seen earlier, but there was also a menacing quality to his expression that sent a chill down her spine. This was the man who'd spent the last decade in the military.

From the wide-eyed, scared look on Vinnie's face, Faith could only assume that whatever Luke was saying was having an impact on her ex-husband.

Luke moved away from Vinnie and the attendants lifted the gurney into the ambulance. She released a sigh of relief when the vehicle rumbled down the drive. A powerful sense of momentary freedom infused her, but did nothing to dispel the ache in her heart.

With the letter in hand, she walked down the stairs and over to where Luke stood talking with the sheriff. Both men turned at her approach and Sheriff Bane tipped his hat before ambling away.

Luke's penetrating gaze caught Faith off guard. She swallowed back the urge to fling herself into his arms and ask him to hold her until she felt safe again. Instead, she said, "Thank you, again."

He nodded, his gaze never wavering. She couldn't ascertain what he was thinking, so with a trembling hand she held out the envelope and felt a part of her shrivel up into a tight ball. He would open the letter and go to wherever he'd been assigned.

For a long moment neither moved. He looked at the envelope then back to her face. His hand reached out and closed over hers. "Faith, I…"

"It's okay, Luke," she interrupted him, wanting to spare him from having to say the words or her from hearing them. "We both knew this moment would come."

She withdrew her hand, leaving the envelope in his grasp. With a heavy heart, she said, "You're—you're free to go back to your life now. I don't need your protection any longer." Just his love.

He nodded, his expression shuttered. "I see."

Do you? she wondered, tears burning the backs of her eyelids. She refused to give in to the pain tearing at her heart. "I'll leave in the morning."

"Whatever you'd like. Just let me know how I can help you," he responded in clipped, formal tones.

Rapidly losing the battle with her tears, Faith nodded and hurried back to the house.

FOURTEEN

Luke knelt beside his bed, his head bowed and eyes closed. *Heavenly Father, I'm asking You for guidance. I know what my heart wants, but I will do what You want.* He waited and listened with his whole being for some reply. Moments passed. *Okay, Lord. Let me be more specific. Do I tell Faith that I love her and ask her to stay even though she's made it clear she wants to leave? Or do I let her go and return to the military?*

He waited for the excitement, the sense of adventure that always came when he thought of his career. They didn't come.

Realization hit him full in the chest. He didn't want to return to his military life. Relief swept away the guilt he'd felt for leaving his men to flounder. He shook his head. They weren't his men, they belonged to God. And now someone else was leading them. *Forgive me, Lord, for being so arrogant.*

But that still left the question of Faith. Would she be content to be a rancher's wife? Did he dare ask her to be?

Lord?

Luke's mouth quirked. Free will. Sometimes the Lord left the decision to His children. Well, he knew what he wanted and the only way to get it was to ask.

Twilight had come and gone. Dusk settled over the ranch, the darkness a relief to the grim events of the day. On Christmas Eve, Faith had expected to be in church singing worship songs, not in her room, fighting off an ache that clenched her stomach into a hard knot. Around her, clothes lay in heaps. Her open suitcase sat on the bed.

For so long, tension and fear had been her constant companions. But now all she felt was a deep, wrenching pain. A tear slipped down her cheek, leaving a wet trail in its wake. She was doing the right thing by not staying at the ranch. She'd already put the Campbells through enough. And this time when she left, she wouldn't be alone. God would walk with her every step of the way.

But she loved Luke. Her heart and her mind knew the truth. And if she didn't tell him, she'd live the rest of her life with regret.

Dear God, I want to be with Luke. It doesn't matter to me if it's on the ranch or a military base somewhere, I just want to be with him. I love him. He's told me You have a plan for my life. Please let it include Luke. I ask this in Your Son's precious name. Amen.

Determination dried her tears and lifted her chin. There was unfinished business between her and Mr.

Campbell and it needed to be resolved now. Tonight. On Christmas Eve.

She stepped into the dimly lit hall and ran straight into a moving object. The world teetered, and for a precarious second she thought she'd find herself on her behind, but two strong arms gathered her close, pulling her up against a hard muscled chest.

She knew those arms, that chest. Knew the heady scent that wrapped around her like a cozy blanket. Savoring the embrace, she tilted her head back to look up into Luke's face.

"Sorry," he said, dropping his arms, leaving her feeling vulnerable and cold.

For a moment silence stretched between them. Faith gathered her courage. "Luke, I—"

"Faith, I—" he said over her.

Laughing softly, she held up a hand. "Please, let me say this."

With a slow nod, he stood perfectly still, his gaze intense. "Luke, I—I just want to be sure you understand that the things I said to—to Vinnie were untrue. I said what I did because—"

He pressed a finger to her lips. "I know."

"You do?" she said against the rough pad of his finger.

His hand moved away, leaving a warm spot on her mouth. She licked her lips, tasting the faint essence of him.

"I'll admit, at the time I was taken by surprise. Hearing those words hurt, but—that lasted only a second. I know you were protecting yourself and I know how you protected my mother. And when you attacked Vinnie, I knew you were protecting me." He placed a hand over his heart. "I can't begin to tell you how that made me feel. You're one courageous lady, Faith."

Ducking her head, she could feel her cheeks heating at his praise. Gently, his finger crooked beneath her chin and tilted her face up. The tender expression on his face knocked the breath from her body like his size had nearly knocked her from her feet.

"I know you want to leave in the morning but I just—I—" He took a quick breath and shifted his feet. "I was doing a lot of thinking tonight. And I came to some conclusions. First and foremost, I have to stop running from who I am. I've become everything I thought I didn't want to be. There's no use denying the truth any longer. I'm a rancher, just like my father."

"Oh, Luke." She knew how much he loved his father.

"Ironic, isn't it? I joined the military to keep from becoming my father and here I am wanting nothing more than to follow my father's path."

"I'm sure he would be proud to know that."

Luke nodded. "Yes, he would have been. He was a wise man. He'd said once that each person had to find their own way home, wherever that home may be. It took me a while, but I've finally come home."

Barely daring to breathe, she asked, "Wh—what about your career?"

He took her hands in his. "I'm not going back. That season of my life is over. God has set me on a new road. I belong here."

"But your ministry?"

"Is not limited to the military. I started something that others can finish. Now, it's time to do good closer to home."

Biting her lip, Faith's mind raced. If he wasn't leaving, did that change things between them? "Luke, I—"

"Faith, please." He squeezed her hands. "Let me finish."

She almost protested, wanting to say the words burning on her tongue, but the agitated look now in his eyes kept her silent. She nodded.

Dropping her hands, he began to pace. Three steps left, pivot, three steps right, pivot. For a long tense moment, Faith watched his restless movements until she couldn't stand it any longer. Softly, she prodded, "Luke, what is it?"

As he passed in front of her, he abruptly stopped, his handsome face intent and his eyes dark in the dim hall. "I know I can't offer you what you had in your old life. You deserve better than being the wife of a rancher and I don't blame you for wanting to leave."

Heart racing, Faith interjected, "But, Luke, I—"

"No, Faith, I need to tell you." He took a shuddering breath. "I don't want you to leave."

Urgently, her heart brimming with tentative hope, she asked, "Why?"

Determination etched in every line, every angle of his body. "Because Faith, these weeks with you have been the best in my life. Because, you fill a void inside of me that I didn't know I had."

She tried to stop the trembling that suddenly

began in her knees. Was he trying to say what she hoped he was saying? Did she dare believe that God would grant her the desires of her heart?

Capturing her hands, he said, "You belong in my life, Faith." He pressed a kiss to her palm. "I love you."

The doubts, the fears, all melted away with the utterance of those three little words. Savoring the joy welling up inside, she closed her eyes. "Luke, I—"

No more words could slip past the tightness in her throat.

He dropped his gaze. "It's—it's all right if you don't feel the same. I understand."

"No, Luke. You don't understand."

In a shaky voice, she told him what was in her heart. "I don't want to leave. Don't you know? I love you, too. I have for so long."

"Are you sure? Do you mean it?"

"Don't ever doubt it," she said fiercely and repeated, "I love you, Luke."

Swiftly, he took possession of her mouth. At once wild and urgent, Faith lost herself in the fire igniting between them until a dark, awful thought intruded. What would happen when Vinnie returned?

Regaining control of herself, she pulled back, breaking the contact.

Eyebrows furrowed in concern, Luke asked, "What's wrong?"

"What about Vinnie?"

"What about him?"

"When he gets out of jail, he'll return with a vengeance." Old fear surfaced, clouding her happiness.

Tenderly, Luke stroked her cheek. "Sweetheart, you don't ever have to worry about him again."

"But how can you be sure?"

He gave a mirthless laugh. "Oh, I made it very clear what would happen if he ever came within a thousand miles of you."

The memory of the fear in Vinnie's eyes as Luke bent over him pricked her curiosity. "What did you tell him?"

"You don't want to know. Let's just say it involved the removal of vital body parts."

Faith gaped. "You didn't."

He shrugged sheepishly. "Well, something to that effect."

Giggling, she shook her head. Amazingly, she believed she'd never have to fear Vinnie again. Not with Luke by her side and God watching over them.

"I know it's not officially Christmas yet, but—" He took her hand and led her down the stairs to the living room.

He went to the tree and picked up a beautifully wrapped present. "Merry Christmas."

Her hands shook as she took the gift. Overwhelmed by his generosity and by her lack of a gift for him, she blinked back sudden tears. "I haven't finished your present."

"Your presence is gift enough," he stated softly.

Love for this man filled her soul to overflowing.

"Go ahead, open it," he urged.

Eager to see what was inside, she quickly dispensed with the wrapping and opened the box. She gasped. "Luke!"

His boyish grin filled her with joy.

She lifted the intricately designed butterfly ornament from where it lay on a bed of tissue. As she lifted it high, the glass, multicolored wings caught the light from the tree and reflected on the walls, filling the room in a kaleidoscope of color.

"It's beautiful!"

"Add it to the tree."

A tear slipped down her cheek as she hung the butterfly on a branch.

Luke gathered her close. "Now we'll have a memory of when you joined our family."

"Joined?"

Luke dropped to one knee. "Marry me, Faith."

No longer able to stand she dropped to her knees. Joy bubbled from the depths of her soul. Looks like God was giving her a Christmas blessing after all.

"Yes, I'll marry you."

* * * * *

Dear Reader,

Thank you for reading *Her Christmas Protector*. I hope you enjoyed Faith and Luke's story as each struggled to understand God's plan for their lives. So often we think our lives are one way and that change won't or shouldn't come, but when we're open to God and His blessings, we find that He knows what's best for us so much better than we do. And how much better could it be to discover that plan at Christmas?

Christmas is such a wonderful time of year. The decorations, the music and the holiday cheer. It can also be a lonely and sad time for those without family or friends. My hope is that we would all be open to God's leading and extend His love to those in need during the joyous time of celebrating Jesus's birth. He came so that all would be saved. He came to love everyone, not a select few. He came at Christmas time.

May your Christmas be filled with cheer, blessings and God's abounding love.

God Bless,

Questions for Discussion

1. What made you pick up this book to read? How did it live up to your expectations?

2. Did you think Faith and Luke were realistic characters? Did their romance build believably? Talk about the secondary characters. What did you like or dislike about the people in the story?

3. Was the setting clear and appealing? Could you "see" where the story took place? How did you imagine it?

4. For Faith, she had to realize that God loved her and was with her, even through the bad times. Can you share an instance when you had a hard time remembering that God loved you and was with you even though it didn't seem as if He was?

5. What was the motive behind Luke's decision to join the military? Discuss a time in your life when you made a decision because of your parents. Was Luke's motivation worthy? How did God use Luke's decision?

6. Do you believe that God would not want someone who is a victim of abuse to stay in a bad situation? Why or why not?

7. Did you notice the scripture in the beginning of the book? What application does it have to your life?

8. Did the author's use of language/writing style make this an enjoyable read? Would you read more from this author? What did you particularly like about the writing?

9. What will be your most vivid memories of this book?

10. What lessons about life, love and faith did you learn from this story?

REQUEST YOUR FREE BOOKS!

2 FREE INSPIRATIONAL NOVELS
PLUS 2
FREE
MYSTERY GIFTS

Love Inspired

YES! Please send me 2 FREE Love Inspired® novels and my 2 FREE mystery gifts (gifts are worth about $10). After receiving them, if I don't wish to receive any more books, I can return the shipping statement marked "cancel." If I don't cancel, I will receive 6 brand-new novels every month and be billed just $4.49 per book in the U.S. or $4.99 per book in Canada. That's a savings of at least 22% off the cover price. It's quite a bargain! Shipping and handling is just 50¢ per book in the U.S. and 75¢ per book in Canada.* I understand that accepting the 2 free books and gifts places me under no obligation to buy anything. I can always return a shipment and cancel at any time. Even if I never buy another book, the two free books and gifts are mine to keep forever.

105/305 IDN FVW5

Name _____ (PLEASE PRINT) _____

Address _____ Apt. # _____

City _____ State/Prov. _____ Zip/Postal Code _____

Signature (if under 18, a parent or guardian must sign) _____

Mail to the **Reader Service:**
IN U.S.A.: P.O. Box 1867, Buffalo, NY 14240-1867
IN CANADA: P.O. Box 609, Fort Erie, Ontario L2A 5X3

**Are you a subscriber to Love Inspired books
and want to receive the larger-print edition?
Call 1-800-873-8635 or visit www.ReaderService.com.**

* Terms and prices subject to change without notice. Prices do not include applicable taxes. Sales tax applicable in N.Y. Canadian residents will be charged applicable taxes. Offer not valid in Quebec. This offer is limited to one order per household. Not valid for current subscribers to Love Inspired books. All orders subject to credit approval. Credit or debit balances in a customer's account(s) may be offset by any other outstanding balance owed by or to the customer. Please allow 4 to 6 weeks for delivery. Offer available while quantities last.

Your Privacy—The Reader Service is committed to protecting your privacy. Our Privacy Policy is available online at www.ReaderService.com or upon request from the Reader Service.

We make a portion of our mailing list available to reputable third parties that offer products we believe may interest you. If you prefer that we not exchange your name with third parties, or if you wish to clarify or modify your communication preferences, please visit us at www.ReaderService.com/consumerschoice or write to us at Reader Service Preference Service, P.O. Box 9062, Buffalo, NY 14269. Include your complete name and address.

LIDIR12

REQUEST YOUR FREE BOOKS!
2 FREE RIVETING INSPIRATIONAL NOVELS
PLUS 2 FREE MYSTERY GIFTS

Love Inspired®
SUSPENSE

YES! Please send me 2 FREE Love Inspired® Suspense novels and my 2 FREE mystery gifts (gifts are worth about $10). After receiving them, if I don't wish to receive any more books, I can return the shipping statement marked "cancel." If I don't cancel, I will receive 4 brand-new novels every month and be billed just $4.49 per book in the U.S. or $4.99 per book in Canada. That's a savings of at least 22% off the cover price. It's quite a bargain! Shipping and handling is just 50¢ per book in the U.S. and 75¢ per book in Canada.* I understand that accepting the 2 free books and gifts places me under no obligation to buy anything. I can always return a shipment and cancel at any time. Even if I never buy another book, the two free books and gifts are mine to keep forever.

123/323 IDN FVXT

Name	(PLEASE PRINT)

Address	Apt. #

City	State/Prov.	Zip/Postal Code

Signature (if under 18, a parent or guardian must sign)

Mail to the **Reader Service:**
IN U.S.A.: P.O. Box 1867, Buffalo, NY 14240-1867
IN CANADA: P.O. Box 609, Fort Erie, Ontario L2A 5X3
**Are you a subscriber to Love Inspired Suspense
and want to receive the larger-print edition?
Call 1-800-873-8635 or visit www.ReaderService.com.**

* Terms and prices subject to change without notice. Prices do not include applicable taxes. Sales tax applicable in N.Y. Canadian residents will be charged applicable taxes. Offer not valid in Quebec. This offer is limited to one order per household. Not valid for current subscribers to Love Inspired Suspense books. All orders subject to credit approval. Credit or debit balances in a customer's account(s) may be offset by any other outstanding balance owed by or to the customer. Please allow 4 to 6 weeks for delivery. Offer available while quantities last.

Your Privacy—The Reader Service is committed to protecting your privacy. Our Privacy Policy is available online at www.ReaderService.com or upon request from the Reader Service.

We make a portion of our mailing list available to reputable third parties that offer products we believe may interest you. If you prefer that we not exchange your name with third parties, or if you wish to clarify or modify your communication preferences, please visit us at www.ReaderService.com/consumerschoice or write to us at Reader Service Preference Service, P.O. Box 9062, Buffalo, NY 14269. Include your complete name and address.

LISDIR12R

REQUEST YOUR FREE BOOKS!

2 FREE INSPIRATIONAL NOVELS
PLUS 2
FREE
MYSTERY GIFTS

Love Inspired

HISTORICAL
INSPIRATIONAL HISTORICAL ROMANCE

YES! Please send me 2 FREE Love Inspired® Historical novels and my 2 FREE mystery gifts (gifts are worth about $10). After receiving them, if I don't wish to receive any more books, I can return the shipping statement marked "cancel." If I don't cancel, I will receive 4 brand-new novels every month and be billed just $4.49 per book in the U.S. or $4.99 per book in Canada. That's a savings of at least 22% off the cover price. It's quite a bargain! Shipping and handling is just 50¢ per book in the U.S. and 75¢ per book in Canada.* I understand that accepting the 2 free books and gifts places me under no obligation to buy anything. I can always return a shipment and cancel at any time. Even if I never buy another book, the two free books and gifts are mine to keep forever.

102/302 IDN FVYH

Name   (PLEASE PRINT)

Address   Apt. #

City   State/Prov.   Zip/Postal Code

Signature (if under 18, a parent or guardian must sign)

Mail to the **Reader Service:**
IN U.S.A.: P.O. Box 1867, Buffalo, NY 14240-1867
IN CANADA: P.O. Box 609, Fort Erie, Ontario L2A 5X3

Want to try two free books from another series?
Call 1-800-873-8635 or visit www.ReaderService.com.

* Terms and prices subject to change without notice. Prices do not include applicable taxes. Sales tax applicable in N.Y. Canadian residents will be charged applicable taxes. Offer not valid in Quebec. This offer is limited to one order per household. Not valid for current subscribers to Love Inspired Historical books. All orders subject to credit approval. Credit or debit balances in a customer's account(s) may be offset by any other outstanding balance owed by or to the customer. Please allow 4 to 6 weeks for delivery. Offer available while quantities last.

Your Privacy—The Reader Service is committed to protecting your privacy. Our Privacy Policy is available online at www.ReaderService.com or upon request from the Reader Service.

We make a portion of our mailing list available to reputable third parties that offer products we believe may interest you. If you prefer that we not exchange your name with third parties, or if you wish to clarify or modify your communication preferences, please visit us at www.ReaderService.com/consumerchoice or write to us at Reader Service Preference Service, P.O. Box 9062, Buffalo, NY 14269. Include your complete name and address.

ReaderService.com

Manage your account online!

- Review your order history
- Manage your payments
- Update your address

*We've designed
the Reader Service website
just for you.*

Enjoy all the features!

- Reader excerpts from any series
- Respond to mailings and
  special monthly offers
- Discover new series available to you
- Browse the Bonus Bucks catalogue
- Share your feedback

Visit us at:
ReaderService.com